ELEVATION

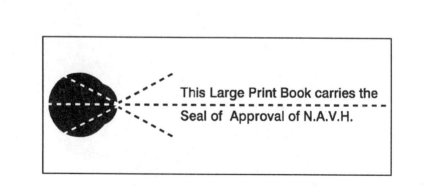

This Large Print Book carries the
Seal of Approval of N.A.V.H.

ELEVATION

STEPHEN KING

THORNDIKE PRESS
A part of Gale, Cengage Learning

GALE
CENGAGE Learning®

Farmington Hills, Mich • San Francisco • New York • Waterville, Maine
Meriden, Conn • Mason, Ohio • Chicago

Thorndike Press® Large Print Core.
The text of this Large Print edition is unabridged.
Other aspects of the book may vary from the original edition.
Set in 16 pt. Plantin.

LIBRARY OF CONGRESS CIP DATA ON FILE.
CATALOGUING IN PUBLICATION FOR THIS BOOK
IS AVAILABLE FROM THE LIBRARY OF CONGRESS

ISBN-13: 978-1-4328-5806-3 (hardcover)

Published in 2018 by arrangement with Scribner, an imprint of Simon & Schuster, Inc.

Printed in the United States of America
1 2 3 4 5 6 7 22 21 20 19 18

Thinking of
Richard Matheson

CHAPTER 1
LOSING WEIGHT

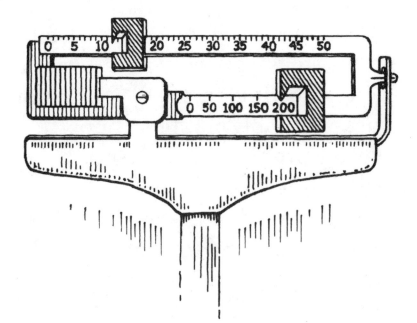

Scott Carey knocked on the door of the Ellis condo unit, and Bob

Ellis (everyone in Highland Acres still called him Doctor Bob, although he was five years retired) let him in. "Well, Scott, here you are. Ten on the dot. Now what can I do for you?"

Scott was a big man, six-feet-four in his stocking feet, with a bit of a belly growing in front. "I'm not sure. Probably nothing, but . . . I have a problem. I hope not a big one, but it might be."

"One you don't want to talk to your regular doctor about?" Ellis was seventy-four, with thinning silver hair and a small limp that didn't slow him down much on the tennis court. Which was where he and Scott had met, and become friends. Not close friends, maybe, but friends, sure enough.

"Oh, I went," Scott said, "and got a checkup. Which was overdue. Bloodwork, urine, prostate, the whole nine yards. Everything checked out. Cholesterol a little high, but still in the normal range. It was diabetes I was worried about. WebMD suggested that was the most likely."

Until he knew about the clothes, that was. The thing with the clothes wasn't on any website, medical or otherwise. It certainly had nothing to do with diabetes.

Ellis led him into the living room, where a big bay window overlooked the fourteenth green of the Castle Rock gated community where he and his wife now lived. Doctor Bob played the occasional round, but mostly stuck to tennis. It was Ellis's wife who enjoyed golf, and Scott suspected that was the reason they were living here, when they weren't spending winters in a similar sports-oriented development in Florida.

Ellis said, "If you're looking for Myra, she's at her Methodist Women's group. I think that's right, although it might be one of her town committees. Tomorrow she's off to Portland for a meeting of the New England Mycological Society. That woman hops around like a hen on a hot griddle. Take off your coat, sit down, and tell me what's on your mind."

Although it was early October

and not particularly cold, Scott was wearing a North Face parka. When he took it off and laid it beside him on the sofa, the pockets jingled.

"Would you like coffee? Tea? I think there's a breakfast pastry, if —"

"I'm losing weight," Scott said abruptly. "That's what's on my mind. It's sort of funny, you know. I used to steer clear of the bathroom scale, because these last ten years or so, I haven't been crazy about the news I got from it. Now I'm on it first thing every morning."

Ellis nodded. "I see."

No reason for *him* to avoid the bathroom scale, Scott thought; the man was what his grandmother would have called a stuffed string. He'd probably live another twenty years, if a wild card didn't come out of the deck. Maybe even make the century.

"I certainly understand the scale-avoidance syndrome, saw it all the time when I was practicing. I also saw the opposite, compulsive weighing. Usually in bulimics and anorexics. You hardly look like one of those." He leaned forward, hands clasped between his skinny thighs. "You *do* understand that I'm re-tired, don't you? I can advise, but I can't prescribe. And my advice will probably be for you to go back to your regular doctor, and make a full disclosure."

Scott smiled. "I suspect my doc

would want me in the hospital for tests right away, and last month I landed a big job, designing inter-locking websites for a department store chain. I won't go into details, but it's a plum. I was very fortunate to get the gig. It's a large step up for me, and I can do it without moving out of Castle Rock. That's the beauty of the computer age."

"But you can't work if you fall ill," Ellis said. "You're a smart guy, Scott, and I'm sure you know that weight-loss isn't just a marker for diabetes, it's a marker for cancer. Among other things. How much weight are we talking about?"

"Twenty-eight pounds." Scott looked out the window and ob-served white golf carts moving over green grass beneath a blue sky. As a photograph, it would have looked good on the Highland Acres website. He was sure they had one — everyone did these days, even roadside stands selling corn and apples had websites — but he hadn't created it. He had moved on to bigger things. "So far."

Bob Ellis grinned, showing teeth that were still his own. "That's a fair amount, all right, but my guess is you could stand to lose it. You move very well on the tennis court for a big man, and you put in your time on the machines in the health club, but carrying too many pounds puts a strain not just on the heart but the whole kit and caboodle. As I'm sure you know. From WebMD."

He rolled his eyes at this, and Scott smiled. "What are you now?"

"Guess," Scott said.

Bob laughed. "What do you think this is, the county fair? I'm fresh out of Kewpie dolls."

"You were in general practice for what, thirty-five years?"

"Forty-two."

"So don't be modest, you've weighed thousands of patients thousands of times." Scott stood up, a tall man with a big frame wearing jeans, a flannel shirt, and scuffed-up Georgia Giants. He looked more like a woodsman or a horse-wrangler than a web designer. "Guess my weight. We'll get to my fate later."

Doctor Bob cast the eye of a

professional up and down Scott Carey's seventy-six inches — more like seventy-eight, in the boots. He paid particular attention to the curve of belly over the belt, and the long thigh muscles built up by leg-presses and hack squats on machines Doctor Bob now avoided. "Unbutton your shirt and hold it open."

Scott did this, revealing a gray tee with UNIVERSITY OF MAINE ATHLETIC DEPARTMENT on the front. Bob saw a broad chest, muscular, but developing those adipose deposits wiseass kids liked to call man-tits.

"I'm going to say . . ." Ellis paused, interested in the challenge now. "I'm going to say 235. Maybe

240. Which means you must have been up around 270 before you started to lose. I must say you carried it well on the tennis court. That much I wouldn't have guessed."

Scott remembered how happy he had been when he'd finally mustered the courage to get on the scale earlier this month. Delighted, actually. The steady rate of the weight-loss since then was worrisome, yes, but only a little. It was the clothes thing that had changed worry to fright. You didn't need WebMD to tell you that the clothes thing was more than strange; it was fucking outré.

Outside, a golf cart trundled past. In it were two middle-aged men, one in pink pants, one in green, both overweight. Scott thought they would have done themselves some good by ditching the cart and walking their round, instead.

"Scott?" Doctor Bob said. "Are you there, or did I lose you?"

"I'm here," Scott said. "The last time we played tennis, I *did* go 240. I know, because that was when I finally got on the scale. I decided the time had come to drop a few pounds. I was starting to get all out of breath by the third set. But as of this morning, I weigh 212."

He sat down again next to his parka (which gave another jingle). Bob eyed him carefully. "You don't look like 212 to me, Scott. Pardon me for saying, but you look quite a bit heavier than that."

"But healthy?"

"Yes."

"Not sick."

"No. Not to look at you, anyway, but —"

"Have you got a scale? I bet you do. Let's check it out."

Doctor Bob considered him for a moment, wondering if Scott's actual problem might be in the gray matter above his eyebrows. In his experience, it was mostly women who tended to be neurotic about their weight, but it happened with men, too. "All right, let's do that. Follow me."

Bob led him into a study stocked with bookshelves. There was a framed anatomy chart on one wall and a line of diplomas on another. Scott was staring at the paper-weight between Ellis's computer and his printer. Bob followed his gaze and laughed. He picked the skull up off the desk and tossed it to Scott.

"Plastic rather than bone, so don't worry about dropping it. A gift from my eldest grandson. He's thirteen, which I think of as the Age of Tasteless Gifts. Step over here, and let's see what we've got."

In the corner was a gantry-like scale upon which two weights, one big and one little, could be moved until the steel beam balanced. Ellis gave it a pat. "The only things I kept when I closed my office down-town were the anatomy chart on the wall and this. It's a Seca, the finest medical scale ever made. A gift from my wife, many years ago, and believe me when I say no one ever accused *her* of being tasteless. Or cheap."

"Is it accurate?"

"Let's just say if I weighed a twenty-five-pound bag of flour on it, and the scale said it weighed twenty-four, I'd go back to Hannaford's and demand a refund. You should take off your boots if you want something close to a true weight. And why did you bring your coat?"

"You'll see." Scott didn't take off his boots but put the parka on instead, to the tune of more jingling from the pockets. Now not just fully dressed but dressed for the outside on a day much colder than this one, he stepped on the scale. "Let 'er rip."

In order to allow for the boots and the coat, Bob ran the counterweight all the way to 250, then worked backward, first sliding the weight, then nudging it along. The needle of the balance bar remained grounded at 240, and 230, and 220, which Doctor Bob would have thought impossible. Never mind the coat and boots; Scott Carey simply looked heavier than that. He could have been off in his estimate by a few pounds, but he had weighed too many overweight men and women to be *this* far off.

The bar balanced at 212 pounds.

"I'll be dipped in pitch," Doctor Bob said. "I need to have this thing recalibrated."

"Don't think so," Scott said. He stepped off the scale and put his hands in his coat pockets. From each, he took a fistful of quarters. "Been saving these in an antique chamber pot for years. By the time Nora left, it was almost full. I must have five pounds of metal in each pocket, maybe more."

Ellis said nothing. He was speechless.

"Now do you see why I didn't want to go to Dr. Adams?" Scott let the coins slide back into his coat pockets with another jolly jingle.

Ellis found his voice. "Let me be sure I have this right — you're getting the same weight at home?"

"To the pound. My scale's an Ozeri step-on, maybe not as good as this baby, but I've tested it and it's accurate. Now watch this. I usually like a little bump-and-grind music when I strip, but since we've undressed together in the club locker room, I guess I can do without it."

Scott took off his parka and hung it on the back of a chair. Then, balancing with first one hand and then the other on Doctor Bob's desk, he took off his boots. Next came the flannel shirt. He unbuckled his belt, stepped out of his jeans, and stood there in his boxers, tee-shirt, and socks.

"I could shuck these as well," he said, "but I think I've taken off enough to make the point. Because, see, this is what scared me. The thing about the clothes. It's why I wanted to talk to a friend who could keep his mouth shut instead of my regular doc." He pointed to the clothes and boots on the floor, then at the parka with its sagging pockets. "How much would you say all that stuff weighs?"

"With the coins? At least fourteen pounds. Possibly as much as eighteen. Do you want to weigh them?"

"No," Scott said.

He got back on the scale. There was no need to move the weights. The beam balanced at 212 pounds.

Scott dressed and they went back to the living room. Doctor Bob poured them each a tiny knock of Woodford Reserve, and although it was only ten in the morning, Scott did not refuse. He took his down in a single swallow, and the whiskey lit a comforting fire in his stomach. Ellis took two delicate birdy sips, as if testing the quality, then tossed off the rest. "It's impossible, you know," he said as he put the empty glass on an endtable.

Scott nodded. "Another reason I didn't want to talk to Dr. Adams."

"Because it would be in the system," Ellis said. "A matter of record. And yes, he'd have insisted you undergo tests in order to find out exactly what's going on with you."

Although he didn't say so, Scott thought *insisted* was too mild. In

Dr. Adams's consulting room, the phrase that had popped into his head was *taken into custody.* That was when he'd decided to keep his mouth shut and talk to his retired medical friend instead.

"You *look* 240," Ellis said. "Is that how you feel?"

"Not exactly. I felt a little . . . mmm . . . *ploddy* when I actually did weigh 240. I guess that's not a real word, but it's the best I can do."

"I think it's a good word," Ellis said, "whether it's in the dictionary or not."

"It wasn't just being overweight, although I knew I was. It was that, and age, and . . ."

"The divorce?" Ellis asked it

gently, in his most Doctor Bobly way.

Scott sighed. "Sure, that too. It's cast a shadow over my life. It's better now, *I'm* better, but it's still there. Can't lie about that. Physically, though, I never felt bad, still worked out a little three times a week, never got out of breath until the third set, but just . . . you know, ploddy. Now I don't, or at least not so much."

"More energy."

Scott considered, then shook his head. "Not exactly. It's more like the energy I have goes further."

"No lethargy? No fatigue?"

"No."

"No loss of appetite?"

"I eat like a horse."

"One more question, and you'll pardon me, but I have to ask."

"Ask away. Anything."

"There's no way this is a practical joke, right? Pulling the leg of the old retired sawbones?"

"Absolutely not," Scott said. "I guess I don't have to ask if you've ever seen a similar case, but have you ever read about one?"

Ellis shook his head. "Like you, it's the clothes that I keep coming back to. And the quarters in your coat pockets."

Join the club, Scott thought.

"No one weighs the same naked as they do dressed. It's as much a given as gravity."

"Are there medical websites you can go on to see if there are any other cases like mine? Even ones that are sort of similar?"

"I can and will, but I can tell you now there won't be." Ellis hesitated. "This isn't just outside my experience, I'd say it's outside *human* experience. Hell, I want to say it's impossible. If, that is, your scale and mine weigh true, and I have no reason to believe otherwise. What happened to you, Scott? What was the genesis? Did you . . . I don't know, get irradiated by something? Maybe get a lungful of some off-brand bug-spray? Think."

"I *have* thought. So far as I can tell, there's nothing. But one thing's for sure, I feel better having talked to you. Not just sitting on it." Scott stood up and grabbed his jacket.

"Where are you going?"

"Home. I've got those websites to work on. It's a big deal. Although I have to tell you, it doesn't seem quite as big as it did."

Ellis walked with him to the door. "You say you've noted a steady weight-loss. Slow but steady."

"That's right. A pound or so a day."

"No matter how much you eat."

"Yes," Scott said. "And what if it continues?"

"It won't."

"How can you be sure? If it's outside of human experience?"

To this Doctor Bob had no answer.

"Keep your mouth shut about this, Bob. Please."

"I will if you promise to keep me informed. I'm concerned."

"That I can do."

On the stoop, they stood side by side, looking at the day. It was a nice one. Foliage was nearing peak, and the hills were burning with color. "Moving from the sublime to the ridiculous," Doctor Bob said, "how are you doing with the restaurant ladies up the street from you? Heard you were having some problems there."

Scott didn't bother asking Ellis where he had heard this; Castle Rock was a small town, and word got around. It got around faster, he supposed, when a retired doctor's wife was on all sorts of town and church committees. "If Ms. Mc-

Comb and Ms. Donaldson heard you calling them ladies, you'd be in their black books. And given my current problem, they're not even on my radar."

An hour later Scott sat in his own study, part of a handsome three-decker on Castle View, above the town proper. A pricier address than he had been comfortable with, but Nora had wanted it, and he had wanted Nora. Now she was in Arizona and he was left with a place that had been too big even when it had been the two of them. Plus the cat, of course. He had an idea she had found it harder to leave Bill than to leave him. Scott recognized that was a little bitchy, but how often the truth was.

In the center of his computer screen, in big letters, were the words HOCHSCHILD-KOHN DRAFT SITE 4 MATERIAL. Hochschild-Kohn wasn't the chain he was working for, had been out of business for nearly forty years, but with a job as big as this one, it didn't hurt to be mindful of hackers. Hence the pseudonym.

When Scott double-clicked, a picture of an old-timey Hochschild-Kohn department store appeared (eventually to be replaced by a much more modern building, belonging to the actual company that had hired him). Below this: *You bring the inspiration, we bring the rest.*

It was this tossed-off tagline that had actually gotten him the job. Design skills were one thing; inspiration and clever sloganeering were another; when they came together, you had something special. *He* was special, this was his chance to prove it, and he intended to make the most of it. Eventually he would be working with an ad agency, he understood that, and they would tinker with his lines and graphics, but he thought that slogan would stay. Most of his basic ideas would also stay. They were strong enough to survive a bunch of New York City hotshots.

He double-clicked again, and a living room appeared on the screen. It was totally empty; there weren't even light fixtures. Outside the window was a greensward that just happened to be part of the Highland Acres golf course, where Myra Ellis had played many rounds. On a few occasions, Myra's foursome had included Scott's own ex-wife, who was now living (and presumably golfing) in Flagstaff.

Bill D. Cat came in, gave a sleepy miaow, and rubbed along his leg.

"Food soon," Scott murmured. "Few more minutes." As though a cat had any concept of minutes in particular, or time in general.

As if I do, Scott thought. Time is invisible. Unlike weight.

Ah, but maybe that wasn't true. You could feel weight, yes — when you were carrying too much, it made you *ploddy* — but wasn't it, like time, basically just a human construct? Hands on a clock, numbers on a bathroom scale, weren't they only ways of trying to measure invisible forces that had visible effects? A feeble effort to corral some greater reality beyond what mere humans thought of as reality?

"Let it go, you'll drive yourself bugshit."

Bill gave another miaow, and Scott returned his attention to the computer screen.

Above the barren living room was a search field containing the words *Pick Your Style!* Scott typed in *Early American,* and the screen came to life, not all at once, but slowly, as if each piece of furniture were being picked out by a careful shopper and added to the whole: chairs, a sofa, pink walls that were stenciled rather than papered, a Seth Thomas clock, a goodwife rag rug on the floor. A fireplace with a small cozy blaze within. The overhead fixture held hurricane lamps on wooden spokes. Those were a little over the top for Scott's taste, but the salespeople he was dealing with loved them, and assured Scott that potential customers would, too.

He could swipe and furnish a parlor, a bedroom, a study, all in Early American. Or he could return to the search field and furnish those virtual-reality rooms in Colonial, Garrison, Craftsman, or Cottage style. Today's job, however, was Queen Anne. Scott opened his laptop and began picking out display furniture.

Forty-five minutes later, Bill was back, rubbing and miaowing more insistently.

"Okay, okay," Scott said, and got up. He went into the kitchen, Bill D. Cat leading the way with his tail up. There was a feline spring in Bill's step, and Scott was damned if he didn't feel pretty springy himself.

He dumped Friskies into Bill's bowl, and while the cat chowed down, he went out on the front porch for a breath of fresh air before going back to Selby wing chairs, Winfrey settees, Houzz highboys, all with the famous Queen

Anne legs. He thought it was the kind of furniture you saw in funeral parlors, heavy shit trying to seem light, but different strokes for different folks.

He was in time to see "the ladies," as Doctor Bob had called them, coming out of their driveway and turning onto View Drive, long legs flashing beneath tiny shorts — blue for Deirdre McComb, red for Missy Donaldson. They were wearing identical tee-shirts advertising the restaurant they ran downtown on Carbine Street. Following them were their nearly identical boxers, Dum and Dee.

What Doctor Bob had said as Scott was leaving (probably wanting no more than to end their meeting on a lighter note) now recurred, something about Scott having a little trouble with the restaurant ladies. Which he was. Not a bitter relationship problem, or a mysterious weight-loss problem; more like a cold sore that wouldn't go away. Deirdre was the really annoying one, always with her faintly superior smile — the one that seemed to say *lord help me to bear these fools.*

Scott made a sudden decision and hustled back to his study (taking a nimble leap over Bill, who was reclining in the hall) and grabbed his tablet. Running back to the porch, he opened the camera app.

The porch was screened, which made him hard to see, and the

women weren't paying any attention to him, anyway. They ran along the packed dirt shoulder on the far side of the Drive with their bright white sneakers scissoring and their ponytails swinging. The dogs, stocky but still young and plenty athletic, pounded along behind.

Scott had visited their home twice on the subject of those dogs, had spoken to Deirdre both times, and had borne that faintly superior smile patiently as she told him she really doubted that their dogs were doing their business on his lawn. Their backyard was fenced, she said, and in the hour or so each day when they were out ("Dee and Dum always accompany Missy and me on our daily runs") they were *very* well-behaved.

"I think they must smell my cat," Scott had said. "It's a territorial thing. I get that, and I understand you not wanting to leash them when you run, but I'd appreciate you checking out my lawn when you come back, and policing it up if necessary."

"Policing," Deirdre had said, her smile never wavering. "Seems a bit militaristic, but maybe that's just me."

"Whatever you want to call it."

"Mr. Carey, dogs may be, as you say, *doing their business* on your lawn, but they're not *our* dogs. Perhaps it's something else that's concerning you? It wouldn't be a prejudice against same-sex marriage, would it?"

Scott had almost laughed, which would have been bad — even Trumpian — diplomacy. "Not at all. It's a prejudice against not wanting to step in a surprise package left by one of your boxers."

"Good discussion," she had said, still with that smile (not maddening, as she might have hoped, but definitely irritating), and closed the door gently but firmly in his face.

With his mysterious weight-loss the farthest thing from his mind for the first time in days, Scott watched the two women running toward him with their dogs loping gamely along in their wake. Deirdre and Missy were talking as they ran, laughing about something. Their flushed cheeks shone with sweat and good health. The McComb woman was clearly the better runner of the two, and just as clearly holding back a bit to stay with her partner. They were paying zero attention to the dogs, which was hardly neglect; View Drive wasn't a hotbed of traffic, especially in the middle of the day. And Scott had to admit that the dogs were good about keeping out of the road. In that, at least, they were well-trained.

Not going to happen today, he thought. It never does when you're prepared. Yet it would be pleasant to wipe that little quirk of a smile off Ms. McComb's —

But it did happen. First one of the

boxers swerved, then the other followed. Dee and Dum ran onto Scott's lawn and squatted side by side. Scott raised his tablet and snapped three quick photos.

That evening, after an early supper of spaghetti carbonara followed by a wedge of chocolate cheesecake, Scott got on his Ozeri scale, hoping as he always did these days that things had finally started going the right way. They had not. In spite of the big meal he had just put away, the Ozeri informed him that he was down to 210.8 pounds.

Bill was watching him from the closed toilet seat, his tail curled neatly around his paws. "Well," Scott told him, "it is what it is, right? As Nora used to say when she came home from those meetings of hers, life is what we make it and acceptance is the key to all our affairs."

Bill yawned.

"But we also change the things we can, don't we? You hold the fort. I'm going to pay a visit."

He grabbed his iPad and jogged the quarter mile to the renovated farmhouse where McComb and Donaldson had lived for the last eight months or so, since opening Holy Frijole. He knew their schedule pretty well, in the offhand way one gets to know one's neighbors' comings and goings, and this would be a good time to catch Deirdre alone. Missy was the chef at the restaurant, and usually left to start dinner prep around three. Deirdre, who was the out-front half of the partnership, came around five. She was the one in charge, Scott believed, both at work and at home. Missy Donaldson impressed him as a sweet little thing who looked at the world with a mixture of fear and wonder. More of the former than the latter, he guessed. Did McComb see herself as Missy's protector as well as her partner? Maybe. Probably.

He mounted the steps and rang the doorbell. At its chime, Dee and Dum began to bark in the backyard.

Deirdre opened the door. She was dressed in a pretty, figure-fitting dress that would no doubt look smashing as she stood at the hostess stand and then showed parties to their various tables. Her eyes were her best feature, a bewitching shade of greeny-gray and uptilted a bit at the corners.

"Oh, Mr. Carey," she said. "How really nice to see you." And the smile, which said how really *boring* to see you. "I'd love to invite you in, but I have to get down to the restaurant. Lots of reservations tonight. Leaf-peepers, you know."

"I won't keep you," Scott said, smiling his own smile. "I just dropped by to show you this." And he held up his iPad, so she could observe Dee and Dum squatting on his front lawn and shitting in tandem.

She looked at it for a long time, the smile fading. Seeing that didn't give him as much pleasure as he had expected.

"All right," she said at last. The artificial lilt had gone out of her voice. Without it she sounded tired and older than her years, which might number thirty. "You win."

"It's not about winning, believe me." As it came out of his mouth, Scott remembered a college teacher once remarking that when someone added *believe me* to a sentence, you should beware.

"You've made your point, then. I can't come down and pick it up now, and Missy's already at work, but I will after we close. You won't even need to turn on your porch light. I should be able to see the . . . leavings . . . by the streetlight."

"You don't need to do that." Scott was starting to feel slightly mean. And in the wrong, somehow. *You win,* she'd said. "I've already bagged it up. I just . . ."

"What? Wanted to get one up on me? If that was it, mission accomplished. From now on Missy and I will do our running down in the park. There will be no need for you to report us to the local authorities. Thank you, and good evening." She started to close the door.

"Wait a second," Scott said. "Please."

She looked at him through the

half-closed door, face expression-less.

"Going to the animal control guy over a few piles of dog crap never crossed my mind, Ms. McComb. Look, I just want us to be good neighbors. My only problem was the way you brushed me off. Refused to take me seriously. That isn't how good neighbors do. At least not around here."

"Oh, we know exactly how good neighbors *do*," she said. "Around *here*." The slightly superior smile came back, and she closed the door with it still on her face. Not before, however, he had seen a gleam in her eyes that might have been tears.

We know exactly how good neighbors do around here, he thought, walking back down the hill. What the hell did that mean?

Doctor Bob called him two days later, to ask if there had been any change. Scott told him things were progressing as before. He was down to 207.6. "It's pretty damn regular. Getting on the bathroom scale is like watching the numbers go backward on a car odometer."

"But still no change in your physical dimensions? Waist size? Shirt size?"

"I'm still a forty waist and a thirty-four leg. I don't need to tighten my belt. Or let it out, although I'm eating like a lumberjack. Eggs, bacon, and sausage for breakfast. Sauces on everything at night. Got to be at least three thousand calories a day. Maybe four. Did you do any research?"

"I did," Doctor Bob said. "So far as I can tell, there's never been a case like yours. There are plenty of clinical reports about people whose metabolisms are in overdrive — people who eat, as you say, like lumberjacks and still stay thin — but no cases of people who weigh the same naked and dressed."

"Oh, but it's so much more," Scott said. He was smiling again. He smiled a lot these days, which was probably crazy, given the circumstances. He was losing weight like a late-stage cancer patient, but the work was going like gangbusters and he had never felt more cheerful. Sometimes, when he needed a break from the computer screen, he put on Motown and danced around the room with Bill D. Cat staring at him as if he'd gone mad.

"Tell me the more."

"This morning I weighed 208 flat. Straight out of the shower and buck naked. I got my hand-weights out of the closet, the twenty-pounders, and stepped on the scales with one in each hand. Still 208 flat."

Silence on the other end for a moment, then Ellis said, "You're shitting me."

"Bob, if I'm lyin, I'm dyin."

More silence. Then: "It's as if you've got some kind of weight-repelling force-field around you. I know you don't want to be poked and prodded, but this is an entirely new thing. And it's big. There could be implications we can't even conceive of."

"I don't want to be a freak," Scott said. "Put yourself in my place."

"Will you at least think about it?"

"I have, a lot. And I have no urge to be a part of *Inside View*'s tabloid hall of fame, with my picture right between the Night Flier and Slender Man. Also, I've got my work to finish. I've promised Nora a share of the money even though the divorce was final before I got the job, and I'm pretty sure she can use it."

"How long will that take?"

"Maybe six weeks. Of course there'll be revisions and test runs that will keep me busy into the new year, but six weeks to finish the main job."

"If this continues at the same rate, you'd be down around 165 by then."

"But still looking like a mighty man," Scott said, and laughed. "There's that."

"You sound remarkably cheery, considering what's going on with you."

"I *feel* cheerful. That might be nuts, but it's true. Sometimes I think this is the world's greatest weight-loss program."

"Yes," Ellis said, "but where does it end?"

One day not long after his phone conversation with Doctor Bob, there came a light knock at Scott's front door. If he'd had his music turned up any louder — today it was the Ramones — he never would have heard it, and his visitor might have gone away. Probably with relief, because when he opened the front door, Missy Donaldson was standing there, and she looked scared half to death. It was the first time he'd seen her since taking the photos of Dee and Dum relieving themselves on his lawn. He supposed Deirdre had been as good as her word, and the women were now exercising their dogs in the town park. If they were allowing the boxers to run free down there, they really might run afoul of the animal control guy, no matter how well-behaved the dogs were. The park had a leash law. Scott had seen the signs.

"Ms. Donaldson," he said. "Hello."

It was also the first time he'd seen her alone, and he was careful not to step over the threshold or make any sudden moves. She looked like she might leap down the steps and run away like a deer if he did. She was blond, not as pretty as her partner, but with a sweet face and clear blue eyes. There was a fragility about her, something that made Scott think of his mother's decorative china plates. It was hard to imagine this woman in a restaurant kitchen, moving from pot to pot and skillet to skillet through the steam, plating veggie dinners and bossing around the help while she did it.

"Can I help you? Would you like to come in? I have coffee . . . or tea, if you prefer."

She was shaking her head before he was halfway through these standard offers of hospitality, and doing it hard enough to make her ponytail flip from one shoulder to the other. "I just came to apologize. For Deirdre."

"There's no need to do that," he said. "And no need to take your dogs all the way down to the park, either. All I ask is that you carry a couple of poop bags and check out my lawn on your way back. That's not too much to ask, is it?"

"No, not at all. I even suggested it to Deirdre. She almost snapped my head off."

Scott sighed. "I'm sorry to hear that. Ms. Donaldson —"

"You can call me Missy, if you like." Looking down and blushing slightly, as if she'd made a remark that might be taken for risqué.

"I would like that. Because all I want is for us to be good neighbors. Most of the folks up here on the View are, you know. And I seem to have gotten off on the wrong foot, although how I could have gotten off on the right one, I don't know."

Still looking down, she said, "We've been here for almost eight months, and the only time you've really talked to us — either of us

— was when our dogs messed on your lawn."

This was truer than Scott would have liked. "I came up with a bag of doughnuts after you moved in," he said (rather weakly), "but you weren't at home."

He thought she would ask why he hadn't tried again, but she didn't.

"I came to apologize for Deirdre, but I also wanted to explain her." She raised her eyes to his. It took an obvious effort — her hands were clenched together at the waist of her jeans — but she did it. "She's not mad at you, really . . . well, she is, but you're not the only one. She's mad at everybody. Castle Rock was a mistake. We came here because the place was almost business-ready, the price was right, and we wanted to get out of the city — Boston, I mean. We knew it was a risk, but it seemed like an acceptable one. And the town is so beautiful. Well, you know that, I guess."

Scott nodded.

"But we're probably going to lose the restaurant. If things don't turn around by Valentine's Day, for sure. That's the only reason she let them put her on that poster. She won't talk about how bad things are, but she knows it. We both do."

"She said something about the leaf-peepers . . . and everyone says last summer was especially good . . ."

"The summer *was* good," she said, speaking with a little more animation now. "As for the leaf-peepers, we get some, but most of them go further west, into New Hampshire. North Conway has all those outlet stores to shop in, and more touristy stuff to do. I guess when winter comes we'll get the skiers passing through on their way to Bethel or Sugarloaf . . ."

Scott knew most skiers bypassed the Rock, taking Route 2 to the western Maine ski areas, but why bum her out more than she already was?

"Only when winter comes, we'd need the locals to pull us through. You know how it is, you must. The locals trade with other locals during the cold weather, and it's just enough to tide them over until the summer people come back. The hardware store, the lumberyard, Patsy's Diner . . . they make do through the lean months. Only not many locals come to Frijole. Some, but not enough. Deirdre says it's not just because we're lesbians, but because we're *married* lesbians. I don't like to think she's right . . . but I think she is."

"I'm sure . . ." He trailed off. That it isn't true? How in hell did he know, when he'd never even considered it?

"Sure of what?" she asked. Not in a snotty way, but in an honestly curious one.

He thought of his bathroom scale again, and the relentless way the numbers rolled back. "Actually, I'm sure of nothing. If it's true, I'm sorry."

"You should come down for dinner some night," she said. This might have been a snide way of telling him she knew he'd never taken a meal at Holy Frijole, but he didn't think so. He didn't think this young woman had much in the way of snideness in her.

"I will," he said. "I assume you do have frijoles?"

She smiled. It lit her up. "Oh yes, many kinds."

He smiled back. "Stupid question, I guess."

"I have to go, Mr. Carey —"

"Scott."

She nodded. "All right, Scott. It's good to talk to you. It took all my courage to come down here, but I'm glad I did."

She held out her hand. Scott shook it.

"Just one favor. If you happen to see Deirdre, I'd appreciate you not mentioning that I came to see you."

"Done deal," Scott said.

The day after Missy Donaldson's visit, while he was sitting at the counter in Patsy's Diner and finishing his lunch, Scott heard someone behind him at one of the tables say something about "that crack-snackin' restaurant." Laughter followed. Scott looked at his half-eaten wedge of apple pie and the scoop of vanilla ice cream now puddling around it. It had looked good when Patsy set it down, but he no longer wanted it.

Had he heard such remarks before, and just filtered them out, the way he did with most overheard but unimportant (to him, at least) chatter? He didn't like to think so, but it was possible.

Probably going to lose the restaurant, she'd said. We'd have to count on the locals to pull us through.

She'd used the conditional tense, as if Holy Frijole already had a FOR SALE OR LEASE sign in the window.

He got up, left a tip under his dessert plate, and paid his check.

"Couldn't finish the pie?" Patsy asked.

"My eyes were a little bigger than

my stomach," Scott said, which wasn't true. His eyes and stomach were the same size they'd always been; they just weighed less. The amazing thing was that he didn't care more, or even worry much. Unprecedented it might be, but sometimes his steady weight-loss slipped his mind completely. It had when he'd been waiting to snap photos of Dee and Dum squatting on his lawn. And it did now. What was on his mind at this moment was that crack about crack-snackers.

Four guys were sitting at the table the remark had come from, beefy fellows in work clothes. A row of hardhats sat in a line on the win-dowsill. The men were wearing orange vests with CRPW stenciled on them: Castle Rock Public Works.

Scott walked past them to the door, opened it, then changed his mind and went to the table where the road crew sat. He recognized two of the men, had played poker with one of them, Ronnie Briggs. Townies, like him. Neighbors.

"You know what, that was a shitty thing to say."

Ronnie looked up, puzzled, then recognized Scott and grinned. "Hey, Scotty, how you doin?"

Scott ignored him. "Those women live just up the road from me. They're okay." Well, Missy was. About McComb he wasn't so sure.

One of the other men crossed his arms over his broad chest and stared at Scott. "Were you in this conversation?"

"No, but —"

"Right. So butt out."

"— but I had to listen to it."

Patsy's was small, but always crammed at lunchtime and filled with chatter. Now the talk and the busy gnash of forks on plates stopped. Heads turned. Patsy stood beside the cash register, alert for trouble.

"Once again, buddy, butt out. What we talk about is none of your business."

Ronnie got up in a hurry. "Hey, Scotty, why don't I walk out with you?"

"No need," Scott said. "I don't need an escort, but I have to say something first. If you eat there, the food is your business. You can criticize it all you want. What those women do in the rest of their lives is *not* your business. Got it?"

The one who had asked Scott if he had been invited into their conversation uncrossed his arms and stood up. He wasn't as tall as Scott, but he was younger and muscular. Red had crept up his broad neck and into his cheeks. "You need to take your loud mouth out of here before I punch it for you."

"None of that, none of that, now," Patsy said sharply. "Scotty, you need to leave."

He stepped out of the diner without argument, and took a deep breath of the cool October air.

There was a knock on the glass from behind him. Scott turned and saw Bull Neck looking out. He raised a finger as if to say *hang on a second.* There were all sorts of posters in Patsy's window. Bull Neck pulled one of them free, walked to the door, and opened it.

Scott balled his fists. He hadn't been in a fist-fight since grammar school (an epic battle that had lasted fifteen seconds, six punches thrown, four of them clean misses), but he was suddenly looking forward to this one. He felt light on his feet, more than ready. Not angry; happy. Optimistic.

Float like a butterfly, sting like a bee, he thought. Come on, big boy.

But Bull Neck didn't want to

fight. He crumpled up the poster and threw it on the sidewalk at Scott's feet. "Here's your girlfriend," he said. "Take it home and jerk off over it, why don't you? Short of rape, it's the closest you'll ever get to fucking her."

He went back in and sat down with his mates, looking satisfied: case closed. Aware that everyone in the diner was looking at him through the window, Scott bent down, picked up the crumpled poster, and walked away toward noplace in particular, just wanting not to be stared at. He didn't feel ashamed of himself, or stupid for starting something in the diner where half of the Rock ate lunch, but all those interested eyes were annoying. It made him wonder why anyone would want to get up on a stage to sing or act or tell jokes.

He smoothed out the ball of paper, and the first thing he thought of was something Missy Donaldson had said: *That's the only reason she let them put her on that poster.* "Them," it seemed, was the Castle Rock Turkey Trot Committee.

In the center of the sheet was a photo of Deirdre McComb. There were other runners, most of them behind her. A big number 19 was pinned to the waistband of her tiny blue shorts. Above them was a tee-shirt with NEW YORK CITY MARATHON 2011 on the front. On her face was an expression Scott would not have associated with her: blissful happiness.

The caption read: *Deirdre Mc-Comb, co-owner of Holy Frijole, Castle Rock's newest fine dining experience, nears the finish line of the New York City Marathon, where she finished FOURTH in the Women's Division! She's announced that she will run in this year's Castle Rock 12K, the Turkey Trot. HOW ABOUT YOU?*

The details were below the caption. Castle Rock's annual Thanksgiving race would take place on the Friday following the holiday, starting at the Rec Department on Castle View and finishing downtown, at the Tin Bridge. All ages were welcome, adult entrance fee five dollars for locals, seven dollars for out-of-towners, and two dollars for those under fifteen, sign up at the Castle Rock Rec Department.

Looking at the bliss on the face of the woman in the photo — runner's high at its purest — Scott understood that Missy hadn't been exaggerating about Holy Frijole's life-expectancy. Not in the slightest. Deirdre McComb was a proud woman with a high opinion of herself, and quick — much too quick, in Scott's opinion — to take offense. Her allowing her picture to be used this way, probably just for that mention of "Castle Rock's newest fine dining experience," had to be a Hail Mary pass. Anything, anything at all, to bring in a few more customers, if only to admire those long legs standing beside the hostess station.

He folded the poster, tucked it into the back pocket of his jeans, and walked slowly down Main Street, looking in shop windows as he went. There were posters in all of them — posters for bean suppers, posters for this year's giant yard sale in the parking lot of Oxford Plains Speedway, posters for Beano at the Catholic church and a potluck dinner at the fire station. He saw the Turkey Trot poster in the window of Castle Rock Computer Sales & Service, but nowhere else until he reached the Book Nook, a tiny building at the end of the street.

He went in, browsed a little, and

grabbed a picture book from the discount table: *New England Fixtures and Furnishings*. Might not be anything in it he could use in his project — where the first stage was nearing completion, anyway — but you never knew. While he was paying Mike Badalamente, the owner and sole employee, he remarked on the poster in the window, and mentioned that the woman on it was his neighbor.

"Yeah, Deirdre McComb was a star runner for almost ten years," Mike said, bagging up his book. "She would have been in the Olympics back in '12, except she broke her ankle. Tough luck. Never even tried out in '16, I understand. I guess she's retired from the major competitions now, but I can't wait to run with her this year." He grinned. "Not that I'll be running with her long, once the starting gun goes off. She'll blow the competition away."

"Men as well as women?"

Mike laughed. "Buddy, they didn't call her the Malden Flash for nothing. Malden's where she originally came from."

"I saw a poster in Patsy's, and one in the window of the computer store, and the one in your window. Nowhere else. What's up with that?"

Mike's smile went away. "Nothing to be proud of. She's a lesbian. That would probably be okay if she kept it to herself — no one cares what goes on behind closed doors — but she has to introduce that one who cooks at Frijole as her wife. Lot of people around here see that as a big old screw you."

"So businesses won't put up the posters, even though the entry fees benefit the Rec? Just because she's on them?"

After having Bull Neck throw the poster from the diner at him, these weren't even real questions, just a way of getting it straight in his mind. In a way he felt as he had at ten, when the brother of his best friend had sat the younger boys down and told them the facts of life. Now as then, Scott had had a vague idea of the whole, but the specifics were still amazing to him.

People really did that? Yes, they did. Apparently they did this, as well.

"They're going to be replaced with new ones," Mike said. "I happen to know, because I'm on the committee. It was Mayor Coughlin's idea. You know Dusty, the king of compromise. The new ones will show a bunch of turkeys running down Main Street. I don't like it, and I didn't vote for it, but I understand the rationale. The town just gives the Rec a pittance, two thousand dollars. That's not enough to maintain the playground, let alone all the other stuff we do. The Turkey Trot brings in almost *five* thousand, but we have to get the word out."

"So . . . just because she's a lesbian . . ."

"A *married* lesbian. That's a deal-breaker for lots of folks. You know what Castle County's like, Scott, you've lived here for what, twenty-five years?"

"Over thirty."

"Yeah, and solid Republican. *Conservative* Republican. The county went for Trump three-to-one in '16 and they think our stonebrain governor walks on water. If those women had kept it on the down-low they would have been fine, but they didn't. Now there are people who think they're trying to make some kind of statement. Myself, I think they were either ignorant about the political climate here or plain stupid." He paused. "Good food, though. Have you been there?"

"Not yet," Scott said, "but I plan to go."

"Well, don't wait too long," Mike said. "Come next year at this time, there's apt to be an ice cream shop in there."

CHAPTER 2
HOLY FRIJOLE

Instead of going home, as he had intended, Scott walked to the town common to page through his new purchase and look at the photos. He strolled along the other side of Main and saw what he now thought of as the Deirdre Poster one more time, in the knit and yarn shop. Nowhere else.

Mike had kept saying *they* and *those women,* but he really doubted that. It was all about McComb. She was the in-your-face half of the partnership. He thought Missy Donaldson would have been happy to keep it on the DL. That half of the partnership would have serious problems saying boo to a goose.

But she came to see me, he thought, and she said a lot more than boo. That took guts.

Yes, and he had liked her for it.

He put *New England Fixtures and*

Furnishings on the park bench, and began to jog up and down the steps of the bandstand. It wasn't exercise he craved, just movement. I've got ants in my pants, he thought. Not to mention bees in my knees. And it wasn't like climbing the steps, more like springing up them. He did it half a dozen times, then went back to his bench, interested to find he wasn't out of breath, and his pulse was only slightly elevated.

He took out his phone and called Doctor Bob. The first thing Ellis asked about was his weight.

"204 as of this morning," Scott said. "Listen, have you —"

"So it's continuing. Have you thought any more about getting serious and really digging into this?

Because a loss of forty pounds, give or take, *is* serious. I still have contacts at Mass General, and I don't think a total soup-to-nuts exam would cost you a dime. In fact, they might pay you."

"Bob, I feel fine. Better than fine, actually. The reason I called was to ask if you've eaten at Holy Frijole yet."

There was a pause while Ellis digested this change of subject. Then he said, "The one your lesbian neighbors run? No, not yet."

Scott frowned. "You know what, there might be a little more to them than their sexual orientation. Just sayin."

"Mellow out." Ellis sounded slightly taken aback. "I didn't mean to step on your corns."

"Okay. It's just . . . there was an incident at lunch. At Patsy's."

"What kind of incident?"

"A little argument. Over them. Doesn't matter. Listen, Bob, how about a night out? Holy Frijole. Dinner. I'll buy."

"When were you thinking?"

"How about tonight?"

"I can't tonight, but I could on Friday. Myra's going to spend the weekend at her sister's down in Manchester, and I'm a lousy cook."

"It's a date," Scott said.

"A man-date," Ellis agreed. "Next you'll be asking me to marry you."

"That would be bigamy on your part," Scott said, "and I will lead you not into temptation. Just do one thing for me — you make the reservation."

"Still sideways with them?" Ellis sounded amused. "Wouldn't it be better to just give it a pass? There's a nice Italian place in Bridgton."

"Nope. I've got my face fixed for Mexican."

Doctor Bob sighed. "I guess I can make the reservation, although if what I'm hearing about that place is true, I hardly think one will be necessary."

Scott picked Ellis up on Friday, because Doctor Bob no longer liked to drive at night. The ride down to the restaurant was short, but long enough for Bob to tell Scott the real reason he had wanted to put off their man-date until Friday: he didn't want to get into a squabble with Myra, who was on church and town committees that had no love for the two women who ran the Rock's newest fine dining experience.

"You're kidding," Scott said.

"Unfortunately not. Myra's open-minded on most subjects, but when it comes to sexual politics . . . let's just say she was raised a certain way. We might have argued, perhaps even bitterly, if I didn't believe shouting matches between husband and wife in old age are undignified."

"Will you tell her you visited the Rock's Mexican-vegetarian den of iniquity?"

"If she asks where I ate on Friday night, yes. Otherwise I'll keep my mouth shut. As will you."

"As will I," Scott said. He pulled into one of the slant parking spaces. "Here we are. Thanks for doing this with me, Bob. I'm hoping it will put things right."

It did not.

Deirdre was at the hostess stand, not wearing a dress tonight but a white shirt and tapered black slacks that showcased those admirable legs. Doctor Bob entered ahead of Scott, and she smiled at him — not the slightly superior one, with the lips closed and the eyebrows raised, but a professionally welcoming one. Then she saw Scott, and the smile went away. She gave him a cool appraisal with those green-gray eyes, as if he were a bug on a microscope slide, then dropped them and grabbed a couple of menus.

"Let me show you to your table."

As she led them to it, Scott admired the decor. It wasn't enough to say McComb and Donaldson had taken pains; this looked like a labor of love. Mexican music — he thought the type they called Tejano or ranchera — played from the overhead speakers. The walls were soft yellow, and the plaster had been roughed up to look like adobe. The sconces were green glass cacti. Large wall hangings featured a sun, a moon, two dancing monkeys, and a frog with golden eyes. The room was twice the size of Patsy's Diner, but he saw only five couples and a single party of four.

"Here you are," Deirdre said. "I hope you enjoy your meal."

"I'm sure we will," Scott said. "It's good to be here. I'm sort of hoping we can start over, Ms. Mc-Comb. Do you think that would be possible?"

She looked at him calmly, but without warmth. "Gina will be right with you, and she'll tell you the specials."

With that she was gone.

Doctor Bob seated himself and shook out his napkin. "Warm packs, gently applied to the cheeks and brow."

"Beg your pardon?"

"Treatment for frostbite. I believe you just took a cold blast, directly to the face."

Before Scott could reply, a waitress appeared — the only waitress, it seemed. Like Deirdre McComb, she was dressed in black pants and a white shirt. "Welcome to Holy Frijole. Could I bring you gentlemen anything to drink?"

Scott asked for a Coke. Ellis opted for a glass of the house wine, then put on his specs for a better look at the young woman. "You're Gina Ruckleshouse, aren't you? You must be. Your mother was my PA when I still had my office downtown, back in the Jurassic Era. You bear a strong resemblance to her."

She smiled. "I'm Gina Beckett now, but that's right."

"Very good to see you, Gina. Give my regards to your mom."

"I will. She's at Dartmouth-Hitchcock now, over on the dark side." Meaning New Hampshire. "I'll be right back to tell you about the specials."

When she returned, she brought appetizers with their drinks, setting the plates down almost reverently. The smell was to die for.

"What have we got here?" Scott asked.

"Freshly fried green plantain chips, and a salsa of garlic, cilantro, lime, and a little green chile. Compliments of the chef. She says it's more Cuban than Mexican, but she hopes that won't keep you from enjoying it."

When Gina left, Doctor Bob leaned forward, smiling. "Seems you've had some success with the one in the kitchen, at least."

"Maybe you're the favored one. Gina could have whispered in Missy's ear that her mother used to labor in your medical sweatshop." Although Scott knew better . . . or thought he did.

Doctor Bob waggled his shaggy white eyebrows. "Missy, eh? On a first-name basis with her, are we?"

"Come on, Doc, quit it."

"I will, if you promise not to call me Doc. I hate it. Makes me think of Milburn Stone."

"Who's that?"

"Google it when you get home, my child."

They ate, and they ate well. The food was meatless but terrific: enchiladas with frijoles and tortillas that had obviously not come from a supermarket package. As they ate, Scott told Ellis about his little set-to in Patsy's, and about the posters featuring Deirdre Mc-Comb, soon to be replaced by less controversial ones starring a flock of cartoon turkeys. He asked if Myra had been on that committee.

"No, that's one she missed . . . but I'm sure she would have approved the change."

With that he turned the conversation back to Scott's mysterious weight-loss, and the more mysterious fact that he appeared not to have changed physically. And, of course, the most mysterious fact of all: whatever he wore or carried that was supposed to weigh him down . . . didn't.

A few more people came in, and the reason McComb was dressed like a waitress became clear: she *was* one, at least tonight. Maybe every night. The fact that she was doing double duty made the restaurant's economic position even clearer. The corner-cutting had begun.

Gina asked them if they wanted dessert. Both demurred. "I couldn't eat another bite, but please tell Ms. Donaldson it was superb," Scott said.

Doctor Bob put two thumbs up.

"She'll be so pleased," Gina said. "I'll be back with your check."

The restaurant was emptying rapidly, only a few couples left, sipping after-dinner drinks. Deirdre was asking those departing how their meals had been, and thanking them for coming. Big smiles. But no smiles for the two men at the table beneath the frog tapestry; not even a single look in their direction.

It's as if we have the plague, Scott thought.

"And you're sure you feel fine?" Doctor Bob asked, for perhaps the tenth time. "No heartbeat arrhythmia? No dizzy spells? Excessive thirst?"

"None of that. Pretty much the

opposite. Want to hear an interesting thing?"

He told Ellis about jogging up and down the bandstand steps — almost *bouncing* up and down them — and how he had taken his pulse afterward. "Not resting pulse, but pretty damn low. Under eighty. Also, I'm not a doctor, but I know what my body looks like, and there's been no wasting in the muscles."

"Not yet, anyway," Ellis said.

"I don't think there's going to be. I think mass stays the same, even though the weight that should go with mass is somehow disappearing."

"The idea is insane, Scott."

"Couldn't agree more, but there

it is. The power gravity has over me has definitely been lessened. And who couldn't be cheerful about that?"

Before Doctor Bob could reply, Gina came back with the slip for Scott to sign. He did so, adding a generous tip, and told her again how good everything had been.

"That's wonderful. Please come again. And tell your friends." She bent forward and lowered her voice. "We *really* need the business."

Deirdre McComb wasn't at the hostess stand when they went out; she was standing on the sidewalk at the foot of the steps and gazing toward the stoplight at the Tin

Bridge. She turned to Ellis and gave him a smile. "I wonder if I could have a word with Mr. Carey in private? It won't take a minute."

"Of course. Scott, I'm going across the street to inspect the contents of the bookshop window. Just give me a honk when you're ready to roll."

Doctor Bob crossed Main Street (deserted as it usually was by eight o'clock; the town tucked in early) and Scott turned to Deirdre. Her smile was gone. He saw she was angry. He had hoped to make things better by eating at Holy Frijole, but instead he had made them worse. He didn't know why that should be, but it pretty clearly was.

"What's on your mind, Ms. Mc-Comb? If it's still the dogs —"

"How could it be, when we now run them in the park? Or try to, at least. Their leashes are always getting tangled."

"You can run them on the View," he said. "I told you that. It's just a matter of picking up their —"

"Never mind the dogs." Those green-gray eyes were all but snapping off sparks. "That subject is closed. What *needs* to be closed is your behavior. We don't need you standing up for us in the local grease-pit, and restarting a lot of talk that had just begun to die down."

If you believe it's dying down, you haven't seen how few shop windows have your picture in them, Scott thought. What he said was, "Patsy's is the farthest thing in the world from a grease-pit. She may not serve your kind of food there, but it's clean."

"Clean or dirty, that's not the point. If standing up needs to be done, *I'll* do it. I — we — don't need you to play Sir Galahad. For one thing, you're a little too old for the part." Her eyes flicked down his shirt front. "For another, you're a little too overweight."

Given Scott's current condition, this jab entirely missed the mark, but he felt a certain sour amusement at her employment of it; she would have been infuriated to hear a man say some woman was a little too old and a little too overweight to play the part of Guinevere.

"I hear you," he said. "Point taken."

She seemed momentarily disconcerted by the mildness of his reply — as if she had swung at an easy target and somehow missed entirely.

"Are we done, Ms. McComb?"

"One other thing. I want you to stay away from my wife."

So she knew he and Donaldson had talked, and now it was Scott's turn to hesitate. Had Missy told McComb that she had gone to Scott, or had she, perhaps in order to keep the peace, told McComb that Scott had come to her? If he asked, he might get her in trouble, and he didn't want to do that. He was no marriage expert — his own being a fine case in point — but he thought the problems with the restaurant were already putting the couple's relationship under enough strain.

"All right," he said. "*Now* are we done?"

"Yes." And, as she had at the end of their first meeting, before closing the door in his face: "Good discussion."

He watched her mount the steps, slim and quick in her black pants and white shirt. He could see her running up and down the bandstand steps, much faster than he could manage even after dropping forty pounds, and as light on her feet as a ballerina. What was it Mike Badalamente had said? *I can't wait to run with her, not that I'll be running with her long.*

God had given her a beautiful body for running, and Scott wished to God she was enjoying it more. He guessed that, behind the superior smile, Deirdre McComb wasn't enjoying much these days.

"Ms. McComb?"

She turned. Waited.

"It really was a fine meal."

No smile for this, superior or otherwise. "Good. I suppose you've already passed that on to Missy by way of Gina, but I'm happy to pass it on again. And now that you've been here, and shown yourself to be on the side of the politically correct angels, why don't you stick to Patsy's? I think we'll all be more comfortable that way."

She went inside. Scott stood on the sidewalk for a moment, feeling . . . what? It was such a weird mix of emotions that he guessed there was no single word for it. Chastened, yes. Slightly amused, check. A bit pissed off. But most of all, sad. Here was a woman who didn't want an olive branch, and he had believed — naively, it seemed — that everyone wanted one of those.

Probably Doctor Bob's right and I'm still a child, he thought. Hell, I don't even know who Milburn Stone was.

The street was too quiet for him

to feel okay about even a short honk, so he went across the street and stood beside Ellis at the window of the Book Nook.

"Get it straightened out?" Doctor Bob asked.

"Not exactly. She told me to leave her wife alone."

Doctor Bob turned to him. "Then I suggest you do that."

He drove Ellis home, and mercifully, Doctor Bob didn't spend any of the trip importuning Scott to check into Mass General, the Mayo, the Cleveland Clinic, or NASA. Instead, as he got out, he thanked Scott for an interesting evening and told him to stay in touch.

"Of course I will," Scott said.

"We're sort of in this together now."

"That being the case, I wonder if you'd come over, perhaps Sunday. Myra won't be back and we could watch the Patriots upstairs instead of in my poor excuse for a man-cave. Also, I'd like to take some measurements. Start keeping a record. Would you allow that much?"

"Yes to the football, no to the measurements," Scott said. "At least for now. Okay?"

"I accept your decision," Doctor Bob said. "That really was a fine meal. I didn't miss the meat at all."

"Neither did I," Scott said, but this wasn't precisely true. When he got home, he made himself a salami sandwich with brown mustard.

Then he stripped and stepped on the bathroom scale. He had declined the measurements because he was sure Doctor Bob would also want a weigh-in each time he checked Scott's muscle density, and he had an intuition — or perhaps it was some deep physical self-knowledge — which now proved to be correct. He had been at a little over 201 that morning. Now, after a big dinner followed by a hefty snack, he was at 199.

The process was speeding up.

Chapter 3
The Wager

That was a gorgeous late October in Castle Rock, with day after day of cloudless blue skies and warm temperatures. The politically progressive minority spoke of global warming; the more conservative majority called it an especially fine Indian summer that would soon be followed by a typical Maine winter; everyone enjoyed it. Pumpkins came out on stoops, black cats and skeletons danced in the windows of houses, trick-or-treaters were duly warned at an elementary school assembly to stay on the sidewalks when the big night came, and only take wrapped treats. The high schoolers went in costume to the annual Halloween dance in the gym, for which a local garage band, Big Top, renamed themselves Pennywise and the Clowns.

In the two weeks or so since his dinner with Ellis, Scott continued to lose weight at a slowly accelerating pace. He was down to 180, a total drop of sixty pounds, but he continued to feel fine, tip-top, in the pink. On Halloween afternoon he drove to the CVS drugstore in Castle Rock's new strip mall, and bought more Halloween candy than he would probably need. Residents of the View didn't get a lot of costumed customers these days (there had been more before the collapse of the Suicide Stairs a few years earlier), but whatever the little beggars didn't take, he would eat himself. One of the benefits of his peculiar condition, aside from all the extra energy, was how he could eat as much as he wanted without turning into a podge. He supposed all the fats might be playing hell with his cholesterol, but he had an idea they weren't. He was in the best shape of his life, despite the deceptive roll hanging over his belt, and his frame of mind was better than it had been since the days when his courtship of Nora Kenner had been in full flower.

In addition to all that, his department store clients were delighted with his work, convinced (fallaciously, Scott was afraid) that the multiple websites he had crafted would turn their bricks-and-mortar business around. He had recently received a check for $582,674.50. Before banking it, he photographed it. He was sitting here in a little Maine town, working from his home study, and he was next door to rich.

He had seen Deirdre and Missy only twice, and from a distance. Running in the park, Dee and Dum on long leashes and not looking happy about it.

When Scott got back from his drugstore errand, he started up his walk, then diverted to the elm tree in his front yard. The leaves had turned, but thanks to the warmth of that fall season, most of them were still on the tree, rustling gently. The lowest branch was six feet over his head, and it looked inviting. He dropped the bag with the candy in it, raised his arms, flexed his knees, and jumped. He caught the branch easily, a thing he couldn't have come close to doing a year ago. No wasting in his muscles; they still thought they were supporting a man who weighed 240. It made him think of old TV footage, showing the astronauts who'd landed on the moon taking ginormous leaps.

He dropped to the lawn, picked up the bag, and went to the porch steps. Instead of walking up them, he flexed again and jumped all the way to the stoop.

It was easy.

He put the candy in a bowl by the front door, and went into his study. He turned on his computer, but didn't open any of the work-files scattered across the desktop. He opened the calendar function instead, and called up the following year. The date numbers were in black, except for holidays and appointments. Those were in red. Scott had marked only one appointment for next year: May 3rd. The notation, also in red, consisted of a single word: ZERO. When he deleted it, May 3rd turned black again. He selected March 31st, and typed ZERO in the square. That now looked to him like the day when he would run out of weight, unless the rate of loss kept speeding up. Which might happen. In the meantime, however, he intended to enjoy life. Scott felt he owed it to himself. After all, how many people with a terminal condition could say they felt absolutely fine? Sometimes he thought of a saying Nora had brought home from her AA meetings: *the past is history, the future's a mystery.*

It seemed to fit his current situation pretty well.

He got his first costumed customers around four o'clock, and the last ones just past sunset. There were ghosts and goblins, superheroes and stormtroopers. One child was amusingly got up as a blue and white post office box, with his eyes peeking out through the slot. Scott gave most of the kids two of the mini-sized candybars, but the mailbox got three, because he was the best. The younger children were accompanied by their parents. The latecomers, a bit older, were mostly on their own.

The last pair, a boy-girl combo who were supposed to be — maybe — Hansel and Gretel, showed up at just after six thirty. Scott gave them each a couple of treats so they wouldn't trick him (around nine or ten, they didn't look particularly tricksy), and asked if they'd seen any others in the neighborhood.

"Nope," the boy said, "I think we're the last ones." He elbowed the girl. "*She* kept wanting to fix her hair."

"What did you get up the street?" Scott asked, pointing to the house where McComb and Donaldson lived. "Anything nice?" It had just occurred to him that Missy might have created some special Halloween treats, chocolate-dipped carrot sticks, or something of that ilk.

The little girl's eyes went round. "Our mother told us not to go there, because those aren't nice ladies."

"They're lesbeans," the boy amplified. "Daddy said so."

"Ah," Scott said. "Lesbeans. I see. You kids get home safe, now. Stay on the sidewalks."

They went on their way, toting their sacks of sugary treats. Scott closed his door and looked into the candy bowl. It was still half full. He thought he'd gotten sixteen or maybe eighteen customers. He wondered how many McComb and Donaldson had gotten. He wondered if they had gotten any.

He went into the living room, turned on the news, saw video of kids trick-or-treating in Portland, and then turned it off again.

Not-nice ladies, he thought. Lesbeans. Daddy said so.

An idea came to him then, the way his coolest ideas sometimes did: almost completely formed, needing nothing but a few tweaks and a little polish. Cool ideas weren't necessarily *good* ideas, of course, but he intended to follow up on this one and find out.

"Treat yourself," he said, and laughed. "Treat yourself before you dry up and disappear. Why not? Just why the fuck not?"

Scott walked into the Castle Rock Rec at nine the next morning with a five-dollar bill in his hand. Sitting at the Turkey Trot 12K sign-up table were Mike Badalamente and Ronnie Briggs, the Public Works guy Scott had last seen in Patsy's. Behind them, in the gymnasium, a morning league was playing pick-up basketball, shirts versus skins.

"Hey, Scotty!" Ronnie said. "How're you doing, m'man?"

"Fine," Scott said. "You?"

"Pert!" Ronnie exclaimed. "Just as pert as ever I could be, although they cut my hours at the PW.

Haven't seen you at Thursday night poker lately."

"Been working pretty hard, Ronnie. Big project."

"Well, you know what, about that thing in Patsy's . . ." Ronnie looked embarrassed. "Man, I'm sorry about that. Trevor Yount, he's got a big mouth, and nobody likes to shut him up when he goes on one of his rants. Apt to get a bust nose for your trouble if you try it."

"That's all right, water under the bridge. Hey, Mike, can I sign up for the race?"

"You bet," Mike said. "The more the merrier. You can keep me company at the back of the pack, along with the kids, the old, and the out of shape. We've even got a blind guy this year. Going to run with his service dog, he says."

Ronnie leaned over the table and patted Scott's front porch. "And don't worry about this, Scotty my boy, they've got EMTs at each 3K mark, and two at the finish line. If you vapor lock, they'll kick-start you."

"Good to know."

Scott paid his five dollars and signed a waiver stating the town of Castle Rock would not be held responsible for any accidents or medical problems he might incur during the seven-and-a-half-mile race. Ronnie scrawled a receipt; Mike gave him a map of the race-course and a number placard. "Just pull off the backing and stick it to your shirt before the race. Give your name to one of the starters so they can check you off and you're good to go."

The number he'd been assigned, Scott saw, was 371, and this was still over three weeks before the big race. He whistled. "You're off to a good start, especially if these are all adult entry fees."

"They're not," Mike said, "but most are, and if this is like last year, we'll end up having eight or nine hundred running. They come from all over New England. God knows why, but our piddling little Turkey Trot has somehow become a big deal. My kids would say it's gone viral."

"Scenery," Ronnie said. "That's

what brings em. Plus the hills, especially Hunter's. And accourse the winner gets to light the Christmas tree in the town square."

"The Rec has all the concessions along the route," Mike said. "As far as I'm concerned, that's the beauty part. We're talking a lot of hotdogs, popcorn, soda, and hot chocolate."

"No beer, though," Ronnie said sadly. "They voted it down again this year. Just like the casino."

And the lesbeans, Scott thought. The town voted down the lesbeans, too. Just not at the ballot box. The town motto seems to be if you can't keep it on the down-low, then out you must go.

"Is Deirdre McComb still planning to run?" Scott asked.

"Oh, you bet," Mike said. "And she's got her old number. 19. We saved it for her special."

Scott took Thanksgiving dinner with Bob and Myra Ellis, plus two of their five grown children — the ones who lived within driving distance. Scott had two helpings of everything, then joined the kids in a spirited game of tag in the Ellises' large backyard.

"He'll have a heart attack, running around after all that food," Myra said.

"I don't think so," Doctor Bob said. "He's prepping for the big race tomorrow."

"If he tries anything more than just jogging in that 12K, he *will* have a heart attack," Myra said, watching Scott chase down one of her laughing grandchildren. "I swan, men in middle age lose all their sense."

Scott went home tired and happy and looking forward to the Turkey Trot the next day. Before bed, he got on the scale and observed without much surprise that he was down to 141. He wasn't losing two pounds a day yet, not quite, but that would come. He turned on his computer and slid Zero Day back to March 15th. He was afraid — it would have been foolish not to be — but he was also curious. And something else. Happy? Was that it? Yes. Probably crazy, but definitely yes. Certainly he felt singled out somehow. Doctor Bob might think *that* was crazy, but Scott thought it was sane. Why feel bad about what you couldn't change? Why not embrace it?

There had been a cold snap in the middle of November, one hard enough to frost the fields and lawns, but the Friday after Thanksgiving dawned overcast and warm for the season. Charlie Lopresti on channel 13 was forecasting rain for later, perhaps heavy, but it hadn't put a dent in Castle Rock's big day, either among the spectators or the contestants.

Scott put on his old running shorts and walked up to the Rec building at quarter of eight, over an hour before the Trot was scheduled to commence, and there was already a huge crowd there, most of them wearing zip-up hoodies (which would be discarded at various points along the route as bodies warmed). The majority were waiting to check in on the left, where signs read OUT OF TOWN RUNNERS. On the right, where the sign read CASTLE ROCK RESIDENTS, there was a short single file. Scott pulled the backing from his number and pasted it on his tee-shirt, above the bulge of his bogus belly. Nearby, the high school band was tuning up.

Patsy Denton, of Patsy's Diner, checked him in and directed him toward the far side of the building, where View Drive started and the race would begin.

"Being local, you could cheat up to the front," Patsy said, "but it's generally considered bad form. You should find the other three hundreds, and stick with them." She eyed his midsection. "Besides, you'll be runnin at the back with the kiddies soon enough."

"Ouch," Scott said.

She smiled. "Truth hurts, doesn't it? All those bacon-burgers and cheese omelets have a way of comin back to haunt a fella. Bear it in mind if you start to feel your chest tightenin up."

As Scott walked over to join the growing crowd of the locals who had checked in early, he studied the little map. The course was a rough loop. Down View Drive to Route 117 was the first three kilometers. The Bowie Stream covered bridge was the halfway point. Then along Route 119, which became Bannerman Road once it crossed the municipal town line. The tenth kilometer included Hunter's Hill, sometimes known as Runners' Heartbreak. It was so steep the kids often went tobogganing there on snow-days, picking up fearsome speed but kept safe by the plowed banks. The last two kilometers were along Castle Rock's Main Street, which would be lined with cheering spectators, not to mention camera crews from all three of the Portland TV stations.

Everyone was milling in groups, talking and laughing, drinking hot coffee or cocoa. Everyone, that was, except for Deirdre McComb, looking impossibly tall and beautiful in her blue shorts and a pair of snow-white Adidas sneaks. She had placed her number — 19 — off-center, high on the left side of her bright red tee-shirt, in order to leave most of the shirt's front visible. On it was an empanada and HOLY FRIJOLE 142 MAIN STREET.

Advertising the restaurant made sense . . . but only if she thought it would do any good. Scott had an idea she might be beyond that now. Surely she knew that "her" posters had been replaced by less controversial ones; unlike the fellow who would be running with his guide dog (Scott saw him near the starting line, giving an interview), she wasn't blind. That she hadn't just said fuck it and dropped out didn't surprise him; he had a pretty good idea of why she was hanging in there. She wanted to stick it to them.

Of course she does, he thought. She wants to beat them all — the men, the women, the kids, and the blind man with his German shepherd. She wants the whole town to watch a lesbean, and a *married* lesbean at that, throw the switch on their Christmas tree.

He thought she knew the restaurant was toast, and maybe she was glad, maybe she couldn't wait to get the hell out of the Rock, but yes, she wanted to stick it to them before she and her wife went, and leave them with that memory. She wouldn't even have to make a speech, just smile that superior smile. The one that said *in your eye, you provincial, self-righteous assholes. Good discussion.*

She was limbering up, first lifting one leg behind her and holding it by the ankle, then the other. Scott stopped at the refreshment table (FREE TO RACERS, ONE TO A CUSTOMER) and got two coffees, paying a buck for the extra one. Then he walked over to Deirdre McComb. He had no designs on her, nor romantic inclinations of any kind, but he was a man, and could not help admiring her figure as she stretched and turned, all the time looking raptly up at the sky, where there was nothing to be seen but slate gray clouds.

Centering herself, he thought. Getting ready. Maybe not for her last race, but maybe for the last one that really means something to her.

"Hello," he said. "It's me again. The pest."

She dropped her leg and looked at him. The smile appeared, as predictable as sunrise in the east. It was her armor. There might be someone behind it who was hurt as well as angry, but she had determined no one in the world would see that. Except, perhaps, for Missy.

Who was not in evidence this morning.

"Why, it's Mr. Carey," she said. "And sporting a number. Also a front porch, and I do believe it's a little bigger."

"Flattery will get you nowhere," he said. "And hey, maybe it's just a pillow under there, something I wear to fool people." He held out one of the cups. "Would you like a coffee?"

"No. I had oatmeal and half a grapefruit at six this morning. That's all I'll take until halfway. Then I'll stop at one of the stands and help myself to a cranberry juice. Now, if you'll pardon me, I'd like to finish my stretches and my meditation."

"Give me a minute," Scott said. "I didn't really come over to offer you a coffee, because I knew you wouldn't take it. I came to offer you a wager."

She had grasped her right ankle in her left hand and was starting to lift it behind her. Now she dropped it and stared at him as if he had grown a horn in the center of his forehead. "What in God's name are you talking about? And how many times do I have to tell you that I find your efforts to . . . I don't know . . . *ingratiate* yourself to me are unwelcome?"

"There's a big difference between ingratiation and trying to be friendly, as I think you know. Or would, if you weren't always in such a defensive crouch."

"I'm *not* —"

"But I'm sure you've got your reasons to feel defensive, and let's not argue semantics. The wager I'm offering is simple. If you win today, I'll never bother you again, and that includes complaining about your dogs. Run them on View Drive all you want, and if they poop on my lawn, *I'll* pick it up, with never a single word of protest."

She looked incredulous. *"If* I win? *If?"*

He ignored this. "If, on the other hand, I win today, you and Missy have to come to my house for dinner. A *vegetarian* dinner. I'm not a bad cook when I put my mind to it. We'll sit down, we'll drink a little wine, and we'll talk. Kind of break the ice, or at least try to. We don't have to be bosom buddies, I don't expect that, it's very hard to change a closed mind —"

"My mind is *not* closed!"

"But maybe we can be real neighbors. I could borrow a cup of sugar from you, you could borrow a stick of butter from me, that kind of thing. If neither of us win, it's a push. Things can go on the way they have."

Until your restaurant closes its doors and you two blow town, he thought.

"Let me make sure I'm hearing this. You're betting you can beat me today? Let me be frank, Mr. Carey. Your body tells me that you're a typical over-indulgent, under-exercised white American male. If you push it, you'll either go down with leg cramps, a sprained back, or a heart attack. You will not beat me today. *Nobody* is going to beat me today. Now please go away and let me finish getting ready."

"Okay," Scott said, "I get it. You're afraid to take the wager. I thought you might be."

She was lifting her other leg now, but she dropped it. "Jesus shined-up Christ on a trailer hitch. *Fine.* It's a bet. Now leave me alone."

Smiling, Scott put out his hand. "We have to shake on it. That way, if you back out, I can call you a welsher right to your face, and you'll have to suck it up."

She snorted, but gave his hand a single hard grip. And for a moment — just one small glimmer of a moment — he saw a hint of a real smile. Only a trace, but he had an idea she had a fine one when she really let it rip.

"Great," he said, then added, "Good discussion." He started away, back to the 300s.

"Mr. Carey."

He turned back.

"Why is this so important to you? Is it because I — because *we* — are a threat to your masculinity somehow?"

No, it's because I'm going to die next year, he thought, and I'd like to put at least one thing right before

I do. It's not going to be my marriage, that's kaput, and it's not going to be the department store websites, because those guys don't understand that their stores are like buggy-whip factories at the start of the automobile age.

But those things he wouldn't say. She wouldn't understand. How could she, when he didn't fully understand himself?

"It just is," he said finally.

He left her with that.

CHAPTER 4
THE TURKEY
TROT

At ten minutes past nine, only a
little late, Mayor Dusty Coughlin

stepped in front of over eight hundred runners stretching back nearly a quarter of a mile. He held a starter pistol in one hand and a battery-powered bullhorn in the other. The low numbers, including Deirdre McComb, were at the front. Back in the 300s, Scott was surrounded by men and women shaking out their arms, taking deep breaths, and munching last bites of power bars. Many of them he knew. The woman to his left, adjusting a green headband, ran the local furniture shop.

"Good luck, Milly," he said.

She grinned and gave him a thumbs-up. "Same to you."

Coughlin raised the bullhorn. *"WELCOME TO THE FORTY-FIFTH*

ANNUAL TURKEY TROT! ARE YOU FOLKS READY?"

The runners gave a yell of assent. One of the high school band members blew a flourish on his trumpet.

"ALL RIGHT, THEN! ON YOUR MARK . . . GET SET . . ."

The mayor, wearing his big politician's grin, raised the starter pistol and pulled the trigger. The bang seemed to echo off the low-hanging clouds.

"GO!"

The ones at the front moved forward smoothly. Deirdre was easy to spot in her bright red shirt. The rest of the runners were packed tightly together, and their start was not so smooth. A couple fell down and had to be helped up. Milly Jacobs was jostled forward into a pair of young men wearing biking shorts and turned-around hats. Scott grabbed her arm and steadied her.

"Thanks," she said. "This is my fourth time, and it's always like this at the start. Like when they open the doors at a rock concert."

The bike-shorts guys saw an opening, shot past Mike Badalamente and a trio of ladies who were talking and laughing as they jogged, and were gone, running in tandem.

Scott drew even with Mike and gave him a wave. Mike skimmed him a salute, then patted the left side of his chest and crossed himself.

Everyone believes I'm going to have a heart attack, Scott thought.

You'd think whatever antic providence decided it would be interesting to make me lose weight could have at least buffed me out a little, but no.

Milly Jacobs — from whom Nora had once bought a dining room set — gave him a sideways grin. "This is fun for the first half hour or so. Then it's heck. By the 8K mark it's hell. If you make it through that part, you catch a little following wind. Sometimes."

"Sometimes, huh?" Scott said.

"Right. I'm hoping for that this year. I'd like to make it all the way. I've only managed that once. Good seeing you, Scott." With that she picked up the pace and pulled ahead of him.

By the time he passed his own house on View Drive, the pack had begun to spread out more and he had running room. He moved steadily and easily at a fast jog. He knew this first kilometer wasn't a fair test of his stamina, because it was all downhill, but so far Milly was right — it was fun. He was breathing easy and feeling good. That was enough for now.

He passed a few runners, but only a few. More passed him, some from the 500s, some from the 600s, and one speed-devil with 721 pasted to his shirt. This comical fellow had a spinning whirligig mounted on his hat. Scott was in no particular hurry, at least not yet. He could see Deirdre on every straight stretch, maybe four hundred yards ahead. Her red shirt and blue shorts were impossible to miss. She was taking it easy. There were at least a dozen runners ahead of her, maybe even two dozen, and that didn't surprise Scott. This wasn't her first rodeo, and unlike most of the amateurs, she would have a carefully thought-out plan. Scott guessed she would allow others to set the pace until the eighth or ninth K, then start pulling ahead of them one by one and not take the lead until Hunter's Hill. She might even make it exciting by waiting until downtown to put on her final burst, but he didn't think so. She would want to win going away.

He felt the lightness in his feet,

the strength in his legs, and resisted the urge to speed up. Just keep the red shirt in your sights, he told himself. She knows what she's doing, so let her guide you.

At the intersection of View Drive and Route 117, Scott passed a little orange marker: **3K**. Ahead of him were the bike-shorts guys, one pounding along on either side of the yellow centerline. They passed a couple of teenagers, and Scott did likewise. The teenagers looked to be in good shape, but they were already breathing hard. As he left them behind, he heard one of them pant, "We gonna let an old fat guy get ahead of us?"

The teens sped up, one passing Scott on either side, both breathing harder than ever.

"Seeya, wouldn't want to be ya!" one of them puffed.

"Go with your bad selves," Scott said, smiling.

He ran easily, eating up the road with long strides. Respiration still okay, ditto heart-rate, and why not? He was a hundred pounds lighter than he looked, and that was only half of what he had going for him. The other half was muscles still built for a man carrying 240.

Route 117 made a double curve, then ran straight beside Bowie Stream, babbling and chuckling along in its shallow, stony bed. Scott thought it had never sounded better, the misty air he was pulling deep into his lungs had never tasted better, the big pines crowding down on the other side of the road had never looked better. He could smell them, tangy and bright and somehow green. Every breath seemed deeper than the last, and he kept having to rein himself in.

I am so glad to be alive on this day, he thought.

Outside the covered bridge crossing the stream, one of those orange markers announced **6K**. Beyond it was a sign reading HALFWAY HOME! The sound of feet thundering inside the bridge was — to Scott, at least — as beautiful as a Gene Krupa drumroll. Overhead, disturbed swallows raced back and forth under the roof. One actually flew into his face, its wing fluttering his brow, and he laughed aloud.

On the far side, one of the bike-shorts dudes was sitting on the guardrail, gasping for breath and massaging a cramp in his calf. He didn't look up as Scott and the other runners passed. At the junction of Routes 117 and 119, runners were clustered around a refreshment table, gulping water, Gatorade, and cranberry juice from paper cups before going on. Eight or nine others, who had blown themselves out on the first six kilometers, were sprawled on the grass. He was delighted to see Trevor Yount — the bullnecked Public Works guy with whom Scott had had the confrontation in Patsy's — was among them.

He passed the sign reading CASTLE ROCK MUNICIPAL TOWN LIMITS, where Route 119 became Bannerman Road, named after the town's longest serving sheriff, an unlucky fellow who had come to a bad end on one of the town's back roads. It was time to pick up the pace, and as Scott passed the orange 8K marker, he shifted from first gear to second. No problem. The air was cool and delicious on his blood-warmed skin, like being rubbed with silk, and he liked the feel of his own heart — that sturdy little engine — in his chest. There were houses on both sides of the road now, and people standing out on lawns, holding up signs and taking pictures.

Here was Milly Jacobs, still going but starting to slow down, her headband darkened to a deeper green with her sweat.

"How's that following wind, Milly? Picking any up?"

She turned to look at him, frankly incredulous. "Good God, I can't . . . believe it's you," she panted. "Thought I left you . . . in the dust."

"I found a little extra," Scott said. "Don't quit now, Milly, this is the good part." Then she was behind him.

The road began to rise in a series of low but ascending hills, and Scott began to pass more runners — both those who had given up and those who were still laboring along. Two of the latter were the teenagers who had blown by him earlier, offended to be passed, even for a few moments, by a middle-aged fatty in shitty sneakers and old tennis shorts. They glanced at him with identical expressions of surprise. Smiling pleasantly, Scott said, "Seeya, wouldn't want to be ya."

One of them gave him the finger. Scott blew him a kiss, then showed them the heels of his shitty sneakers.

As Scott entered the ninth kilometer, a long peal of thunder rolled across the sky, west to east.

That's not good, he thought. November thunder might be okay

in Louisiana, but not in Maine.

He came around a bend, jinking left to come even with a skinny old stork of a man who was running with his fists clenched before him and his head thrown back. His wifebeater shirt showed fishbelly white arms decorated with old tattoos. On his face he wore a daffy grin. "You hear that thunder?"

"Yes!"

"Gonna rain a bitch! Ain't this a day?"

"You bet your ass," Scott said, laughing. "Finest kind!" Then he was past, but not before the skinny old guy gave him a pretty good swat on the ass.

The road ran straight now, and Scott spotted the red shirt and blue shorts halfway up Hunter's Hill, aka Runners' Heartbreak. He could see only half a dozen runners ahead of McComb now. There might already be a couple beyond the crest of the hill, but Scott doubted it.

It was time to shift into a higher gear.

He did so, and was now among the serious runners, the greyhounds. But many of them were either beginning to flag or saving their energy for the steep grade. He caught unbelieving looks as the middle-aged man with his belly pushing out his sweaty tee-shirt first wove his way among them, then put them behind him.

Partway up Hunter's Hill, Scott's breath began to shallow up, and the air going in and out began to taste hot and coppery. His feet no longer felt so light, and his calves were burning. There was a dull ache on the left side of his groin, as if he had strained something there. The second half of the hill looked endless. He thought about what Milly had said: first fun, then heck, then hell. Was he in heck or hell now? On the border, he decided.

He had never really assumed he could beat Deirdre McComb (although he hadn't discounted the possibility), but he *had* assumed he would finish the race somewhere near the front — that the muscles built to carry his earlier, heavier self would be enough to bring him through. Now, as he passed a couple of runners who had given up, one sitting with his head bent, the other lying on his back and gasping, he began to wonder about that.

Maybe I still weigh too much, he thought. Or maybe I just don't have the sack for this.

There was another roll of thunder.

Because the top of Hunter's didn't seem to be getting any closer, he looked down at the road, watching the pebbles set in the macadam flying past like galaxies in a science fiction movie. He looked up just in time to keep from crashing into a redhead who was standing with one foot on either side of the yellow line, holding onto her knees and gasping. Scott barely avoided her and saw the crest of the hill sixty yards ahead. Also one of those orange markers: **10K.** He fixed his eyes on it and ran, now not just gasping for breath but *yanking* for it, and feeling every one of his forty-two years. His left knee began to complain, pulsing in sync with the pain in his groin. Sweat ran down his cheeks like hot water.

You are going to do this. You *will* do this. Put it all on the line.

And why the fuck not? If Zero Day turned out to be today instead of in February or March, so be it.

He passed the marker and crested the hill. Purdy's Lumberyard was on the right, Purdy's Hardware on the left. Just two klicks to go. He could see downtown below him, twenty or so businesses on either side hung with bunting, the Catholic church and the Methodist one facing off like holy gunslingers, the slant parking (every space taken), the clogged sidewalks, and the town's two stoplights. Beyond the second one was the Tin Bridge, where bright yellow finishing tape decorated with turkeys had been strung. Ahead of Scott he now saw only six or seven runners. The one in the red shirt was second, and closing the distance on the leader. Deirdre was making her move.

I'm never going to catch her, Scott thought. She's got too much of a lead. That damn hill didn't break me, but it bent me pretty good.

Then his lungs seemed to open up again, each breath going deeper than the one before. His sneakers (not blinding white Adidas, just ratty old Pumas) seemed to shed the lead coating they had gained. His previous lightness of body came rushing back. It was what Milly had called the following wind, and what pros like McComb no doubt called the runner's high. Scott preferred that. He remembered that day in his yard, flexing his knees, leaping, and catching the branch of the tree. He remembered running up and down the bandstand steps. He remembered dancing across the kitchen floor as Stevie Wonder sang "Superstition."

This was the same. Not a wind, not even a high, exactly, but an elevation. A sense that you had gone beyond yourself and could go farther still.

Heading down Hunter's, past O'Leary Ford on one side and Zoney's Go-Mart on the other, he passed one runner, then another. Four back now. He didn't know or care if they were staring as he blew past them. All of his attention was focused on the red shirt and blue shorts.

Deirdre took the lead. As she did, more thunder banged overhead — God's starter pistol — and Scott felt the first cold splat of rain on the back of his neck. Then another on his arm. He looked down and saw more hitting the road, darkening it in dime-sized drops. Now there were spectators on either side of Main, although they still had to be a mile from the finish and half a mile from where the downtown sidewalks started. Scott saw umbrellas popping open like flowers blooming. They were gorgeous. Everything was — the darkening sky, the pebbles in the road, the orange of the marker announcing the Turkey Trot's last K. The world stood forth.

Ahead of him, a runner abruptly swerved off the road, went to his knees, and rolled over on his back, looking up into the rain with his mouth drawn down in a bow of agony. Only two runners between him and Deirdre.

Scott blew past the final orange marker. Just a kilometer to go now, less than a mile. He had gone from first gear to second. Now, as the sidewalks began — cheering crowds on either side, some waving Turkey Trot pennants — it was time to see if he had not just third gear but an overdrive.

Kick it, you son of a bitch, he thought, and picked up the pace.

The rain seemed to hesitate for a moment, time enough for Scott to think it was going to hold off until the race was over, and then it came in a full-force torrent, driving the spectators back under awnings and into doorways. Visibility dropped to twenty percent, then to ten, then to almost zero. Scott thought the cold rain felt more than delicious; closer to divine.

He got by one runner, then another. The second was the former leader, the one that Deirdre had passed. He had slowed down to a walk, splashing along the gushing street with his head down, his hands on his hips, and his sopping shirt plastered to his body.

Ahead, through a gray curtain of rain, Scott saw the red shirt. He thought he had just enough gas left in the tank to go by her, but the race might be over before he could. The traffic light at the end of Main Street had disappeared. So had the Tin Bridge, and the yellow tape across its near end. It was just him and McComb now, both of them running blind through the deluge, and Scott had never been happier in his life. Only happiness was too mild. Here, as he explored the farthest limits of his stamina, was a new world.

Everything leads to this, he thought. To this elevation. If it's how dying feels, everyone should be glad to go.

He was close enough to see Deirdre McComb look back, her sodden ponytail doing a dead-fish flop onto her shoulder as she did it. Her eyes widened when she saw who was trying to take away her lead. She faced forward, lowered her head, and found more speed.

Scott first matched her, then overmatched her. Closing in, closing in, now almost close enough to touch the back of her soaked shirt, able to see clear rivulets of rain running down the back of her neck. Able — even over the roar of the storm — to hear her gasping air out of the rain. He could see her, but not the buildings they were passing on either side, or the last stoplight, or the bridge. He had lost all sense of where he was on Main, and had no landmarks to help him. His only landmark was the red shirt.

She looked back again, and that was a mistake. Her left foot caught her right ankle and she went down, arms out, surfing water up in front and splashing to either side like a kid bellyflopping into a swimming pool. He heard her grunt as the air went out of her.

Scott reached her, stopped, bent down. She twisted up on one arm to look at him. Her face was an agony of fury and hurt. "How did you cheat?" she gasped. "Goddam you, how did you ch—"

He grabbed her. Lightning flashed, a brief glare that made him wince. "Come on." He put his other arm around her waist and hauled her up.

Her eyes went wide. There was another flash of lightning. "Oh my God, what are you doing? *What's happening to me?*"

He ignored this. Her feet moved, but not on the street, which was now an inch deep in running water;

they pedaled in the air. He knew what was happening to her, and he was sure it was amazing, but it wasn't happening to him. She was light to herself, maybe more than light, but heavy to him, a slim body that was all muscle and sinew. He let loose. He still couldn't see the Tin Bridge, but he could see a faint yellow streak that had to be the tape.

"Go!" he shouted, and pointed at the finish line. *"Run!"*

She did. He ran after her. She broke the tape. Lightning flashed. He followed, raising his hands into the rain, slowing down as he ran onto the Tin Bridge. He found her halfway across on her hands and knees. He dropped down beside her, both of them gasping in air that seemed to be mostly liquid.

She looked at him, water running down her face like tears.

"What happened? My God, you put your arm around me and it was like I weighed nothing!"

Scott thought of the coins he had put in the pockets of his parka on the day he'd first gone to see Doctor Bob. He thought about standing on his bathroom scale while holding a pair of twenty-pound handweights.

"You did," he said.

"DeeDee! *DeeDee!*"

It was Missy, running toward them. She held out her arms. Deirdre splashed to her feet and embraced her wife. They staggered and almost went down. Scott put his arms out to catch them, but didn't actually touch them. Lightning flashed.

Then the crowd found them, and they were surrounded by the people of Castle Rock, applauding in the rain.

CHAPTER 5
AFTER THE RACE

That evening Scott was lying in a
tub filled with water as hot as he

could stand it, trying to soothe the ache out of his muscles. When his phone began to ring, he fumbled for it under the clean clothes folded on the chair by the tub. I'm tied to this damn thing, he thought.

"Hello?"

"Deirdre McComb, Mr. Carey. What night shall I set aside for our dinner? Next Monday would be good, because the restaurant is closed on Mondays."

Scott smiled. "I think you misunderstood the wager, Ms. McComb. You won, and your dogs now have free rein on my lawn, in perpetuity."

"We both know that isn't exactly true," she said. "In fact, you threw the race."

"You deserved to win."

She laughed. It was the first one he'd heard from her, and it was charming. "My high school running coach would tear his hair out if he heard such a sentiment. He used to say what you deserve has nothing to do with where you finish. I will take the win, however, if you invite us to dinner."

"Then I'll brush up on my vegetarian cooking. Next Monday works for me, but only if you bring your wife. Sevenish, say?"

"That's fine, and she wouldn't miss it. Also . . ." She hesitated. "I want to apologize for what I said. I know you didn't cheat."

"No apology necessary," Scott said, and he meant it. Because, in a way he had cheated, involuntary as it might have been.

"If not for that, I need to apologize for how I've treated you. I could plead extenuating circumstances, but Missy tells me there are none, and she might be right about that. I have certain . . . attitudes . . . and changing them hasn't been easy."

He couldn't think of what to say to that, so he changed the subject. "Are either of you gluten-free? Lactose-intolerant? Let me know, so I don't make something you or Missy — Ms. Donaldson — can't eat."

She laughed again. "We don't eat meat or fish, and that's it. Everything else is on the table."

"Even eggs?"

"Even eggs, Mr. Carey."

"Scott. Call me Scott."

"I will. And I'm Deirdre. Or DeeDee, to avoid confusion with Dee the dog." She hesitated. "When we come to dinner, can you explain what happened when you pulled me up? I've had strange sensations while I'm running, strange perceptions, every runner will tell you the same —"

"I had a few myself," Scott said. "From Hunter's Hill on, things got very . . . weird."

"But I've never felt anything like that. For a few seconds it was like I was on the space station, or something."

"Yes, I can explain. But I'd like to

invite my friend Dr. Ellis, who already knows. And his wife, if she's available." If she'll come, was what Scott didn't want to say.

"Fine. Until Monday, then. Oh, and be sure to look at the *Press-Herald*. The story won't be in the newspaper until tomorrow, of course, but it's online now."

Sure it is, Scott thought. In the twenty-first century, print newspapers are also buggy-whip factories.

"I'll do that."

"Did you think it was lightning? There at the end?"

"Yes," Scott said. What else would it have been? Lightning went with thunder like peanut butter went with jelly.

"So did I," DeeDee McComb said.

He dressed and fired up his computer. The story was on the *Press-Herald*'s homepage, and he was sure it would be on the front page of Saturday's paper, maybe above the fold, barring any new world crisis. The headline read: **LOCAL RESTAURANT OWNER WINS CASTLE ROCK TURKEY TROT.** According to the paper, it was the first time a town resident had won the race since 1989. There were only two photographs in the online edition, but Scott guessed there would be more in Saturday's print version. It hadn't been lightning at the end; it had been the newspaper photographer, and he'd gotten class-A pix despite the rain.

The first one showed Deirdre and Scott together, with the Tin Bridge stoplight a smeary red in the background, which meant she must have fallen not even seventy yards from the finish. He had his arm around her waist. Hair that had come loose from her ponytail was plastered to her cheeks. She was looking up at him with exhausted wonder. He was looking down at her . . . and smiling.

SHE GOT BY WITH A LITTLE HELP FROM A FRIEND, the caption read, and below that: *Fellow Castle Rocker Scott Carey helps Deirdre McComb to her feet after she took a spill on the wet road just* *short of the finish line.*

The second photo was captioned **VICTORY HUG,** and named the three people in the picture: Deirdre McComb, Melissa Donaldson, and Scott Carey. Deirdre and Missy were embracing. Although Scott hadn't actually touched them, only raised his arms and curled them around the women in an instinctive gesture to catch them if they fell, he looked like he was joining the hug.

The body of the story named the restaurant Deirdre McComb ran with "her partner," and quoted a review that had run in the paper back in August, calling the food "veggie cuisine with Tex-Mex flair that has to be experienced; this is a trip worth making."

Bill D. Cat had taken his usual position when Scott was at his desktop, perched on an endtable and watching his pet human with inscrutable green eyes.

"Tell you what, Bill," Scott said. "If that doesn't bring in customers, nothing will."

He went into the bathroom and stepped on the scale. Its news didn't surprise him. He was down to 137. It might have been the day's exertions, but he didn't actually believe that. What he believed was that by booting his metabolism into a higher gear (and overdrive at the end), he had sped the process up even more.

It was starting to look like Zero

Day might come weeks earlier than he had anticipated.

Myra Ellis did come to dinner with her husband. She was timid at first — almost skittish — and so was Missy Donaldson, but a glass of Pinot (which Scott served with cheese, crackers, and olives) loosened both ladies up. And then, a miracle — they discovered they were both mycologically inclined, and spent most of the meal talking about edible mushrooms.

"You know so much about them!" Myra exclaimed. "May I ask if you went to culinary school?"

"I did. After I met DeeDee, but long before we were married. I went to ICE. That's —"

"The Institute of Culinary Education in New York!" Myra exclaimed. A few crumbs tumbled onto her frilly silk blouse. She didn't notice. "It's famous! Oh my God, I'm so *jealous*!"

Deirdre was looking at them and smiling. Doctor Bob was, too. So that was good.

Scott had spent the morning at the local Hannaford's, with Nora's left-behind copy of *The Joy of Cooking* propped open in the child seat of his grocery cart. He asked many questions, and research paid off, as it usually did. He served vegetarian lasagna Florentine with garlic toast points. He was gratified — but not surprised — to see Deirdre put away not one or two but three big slices. She was still in post-run mode, and stuffing carbs.

"For dessert it's only store-bought pound cake," he said, "but the chocolate whipped cream I made myself."

"I haven't had that since I was a kid," Doctor Bob said. "My mom made it for special occasions. We kids called it choco-cream. Bring it on, Scott."

"Plus Chianti," Scott said.

Deirdre applauded. She was flushed, her eyes sparkling, a woman with every part of her body clearly operating in top form. "Bring that on, too!"

It was a fine meal, and the first time he'd pulled out all the stops in the kitchen since Nora had decamped. As he watched them eat and listened to them talk, he realized how empty this house had been with just him and Bill to ramble around in it.

The five of them demolished the pound cake. As Scott began to collect the plates, both Myra and Missy rose. "Let us do that," Myra said. "You cooked."

"Not at all, ma'am," Scott said. "I'm just going to put everything on the counter and load up the dishwasher later on."

He took the dessert plates into the kitchen and stacked them on the counter. He turned and Deirdre was standing there, smiling.

"If you ever want a job, Missy's looking for a sous chef."

"I don't think I could keep up with her," Scott said, "but I'll keep it in mind. How was business over the weekend? Must have been good if Missy's looking for help."

"Sold out," she said. "Every table. People from away, but also people from the Rock that I've never seen before, at least not in our place. And we're booked solid for the next nine or ten days. This is like opening all over again, when people come to see what you've got. If what you've got isn't tasty, or even just so-so, most don't try again. But what Missy makes is a lot more than so-so. They *will* come back."

"Winning the race made a difference, huh?"

"The *pictures* were what made

the difference. And without you, the pictures would have just been a dyke winning a footrace, big deal."

"You're too hard on yourself."

She shook her head, smiling. "I don't think so. Brace yourself, big boy, I'm coming in for a hug."

She stepped forward. Scott stepped back, holding his hands out, palms forward. Her face clouded.

"It's not you," he said. "Believe me, I'd love nothing more than to hug you. We both deserve it. But it might not be safe."

Missy was standing in the kitchen doorway with wineglasses held between her fingers by the stems. "What is it, Scott? Is something wrong with you?"

He grinned. "You might say."

Doctor Bob joined the women. "Are you going to tell them?"

"Yes," Scott said. "In the living room."

He told them everything. The relief was enormous. Myra only looked puzzled, as if she hadn't quite taken it in, but Missy was disbelieving.

"It's not possible. People's bodies change when they lose weight, that's just a fact."

Scott hesitated, then went to where she was sitting next to Deirdre on the couch. "Give me your hand. Just for a second."

She held it out with no hesitation. Total trust. This much can't hurt, he told himself, and hoped it was true. He had pulled Deirdre to her feet when she'd fallen, after all, and she was all right.

He took Missy's hand and pulled. She flew up from the couch, her hair streaming out behind her and her eyes wide. He caught her to keep her from crashing into him, lifted her, set her down, and stepped back. Her knees flexed when his hands left her and weight came back into her body. Then she stood, staring at him in amazement.

"You . . . I . . . *Jesus!*"

"What was it like?" Doctor Bob asked. He was sitting forward in his chair, eyes bright. "Tell me!"

"It was . . . well . . . I don't think I can."

"Try," he urged.

"It was a little like being on a rollercoaster when it goes over the top of the first steep hill and starts down. My stomach went up . . ." She laughed shakily, still staring at Scott. "*Everything* went up!"

"I tried it with Bill," Scott said, and nodded to where his cat was currently stretched out on the brick hearth. "He freaked out. Laddered scratches up my arm in his hurry to jump down, and Bill never scratches."

"Anything you take hold of has no weight?" Deirdre said. "Is that really true?"

Scott thought about this. He had thought about it often, and sometimes it seemed to him that what was happening to him wasn't a phenomenon but something like a germ, or a virus.

"Living things have no weight. To *them,* at least, but —"

"They have weight to you."

"Yes."

"But other things? Inanimate objects?"

"Once I pick them up . . . or wear them . . . no. No weight." He shrugged.

"How can that be?" Myra asked. "How can that possibly be?" She looked at her husband. "Do you know?"

He shook his head.

"How did it start?" Deirdre asked. "What caused it?"

"No idea. I don't even know *when*

it started, because I wasn't in the habit of weighing myself until the process was already under way."

"In the kitchen you said it wasn't safe."

"I said it might not be. I don't know for sure, but that sort of sudden weightlessness might screw up your heart . . . your blood-pressure . . . your brain function . . . who knows?"

"Astronauts are weightless," Missy objected. "Or almost. I guess those circling the earth must still be subject to at least some gravitational pull. And the ones who walked on the moon, as well."

"It isn't just that, is it?" Deirdre said. "You're afraid it might be contagious."

Scott nodded. "The idea has crossed my mind."

There was a moment of silence, while all of them tried to digest the indigestible. Then Missy said, "You have to go to a clinic! You have to be examined! Let the doctors who . . . who know about this sort of thing . . ."

She trailed off, recognizing the obvious: there were no doctors who knew about this sort of thing.

"They might be able to find a way to reverse it," she said eventually. She turned to Ellis. "You're a doctor. Tell him!"

"I have," Doctor Bob said. "Many times. Scott refuses. At first I thought that was wrong of him — wrong*headed* — but I've changed my mind. I doubt very much if this is something that can be scientifically investigated. It may stop on its own . . . even reverse itself . . . but I don't think the best doctors in the world could understand it, let alone affect it in any way, positive or negative."

"And I have no desire to spend the remainder of my weight-loss program in a hospital room or a government facility, being examined," Scott said.

"Or as a public curiosity, I suppose," Deirdre said. "I get that. Perfectly."

Scott nodded. "So you'll understand when I ask you to promise that what's been said in this room has to stay in this room."

"But what will happen to you?" Missy burst out. "What will happen to you when you have no weight left?"

"I don't know."

"How will you *live*? You can't just . . . just . . ." She looked around wildly, as if hoping for someone to finish her thought. No one did. "You can't just float along the *ceiling*!"

Scott, who had already thought of a life like that, only shrugged again.

Myra Ellis leaned forward, her hands so tightly clasped the knuckles were white. "Are you very frightened? I suppose you must be."

"That's the thing," Scott said. "I'm not. I was at the very begin-

ning, but now . . . I don't know . . .
it seems sort of okay."

There were tears in Deirdre's
eyes, but she smiled. "I think I get
that, too," she said.

"Yes," he said. "I believe you do."

He thought that if any of them
found it impossible to keep his
secret, it would be Myra Ellis, with
her church groups and committees.
But she *did* keep it. All of them did.
They became a kind of cabal, getting together once a week at Holy
Frijole, where Deirdre always kept
a table reserved for them, with a
little placard on it that said *Dr. Ellis
Party.* The place was always full, or
nearly, and Deirdre said that after
the new year, if things didn't slow

down, they would have to open earlier and institute a second sitting. Missy had indeed hired a sous chef to help her in the kitchen, and on Scott's advice, she hired someone local — Milly Jacobs's oldest daughter.

"She's a little slow," Missy said, "but she's willing to learn, and by the time the summer people come back, she'll be fine. You'll see."

Then she blushed and looked down at her hands, realizing Scott might not be around when the summer people came back.

On December 10th, Deirdre McComb lit the big Christmas tree in the Castle Rock town square. Almost a thousand people turned out for the evening ceremony, which included the high school chorus singing seasonal songs. Mayor Coughlin, dressed as Santa Claus, arrived by helicopter.

There was applause when Deirdre mounted the podium, and a roar of approval when she proclaimed the thirty-foot spruce as "the best Christmas tree in the best town in New England."

The lights came on, the neon angel at the top twirled and curtseyed, and the crowd sang along with the high schoolers: Christmas tree, O Christmas tree, how lovely are your branches. Scott was amused to see Trevor Yount singing and applauding along with everyone else.

On that day, Scott Carey weighed 114 pounds.

CHAPTER 6
THE INCREDIBLE
LIGHTNESS OF
BEING

There were limits to what Scott had come to think of as "the weightless effect." His clothes did not float up from his body. Chairs did not levitate when he sat in them, although if he carried one into the bathroom and stood on the scale with it, its weight didn't register. If there were rules to what was going on, he didn't understand them, or care to. His outlook remained optimistic, and he slept through the night. Those were the things he cared about.

He called Mike Badalamente on New Year's Day, passed on the appropriate good wishes, and then said he was thinking about making a trip to California in a few weeks, to see his only surviving aunt. If he made the trip, would Mike take his cat?

"Well, I don't know," Mike said.

"Maybe. Does he do his business in a litter box?"

"Absolutely."

"Why me?"

"Because I believe every bookstore should have a resident cat, which you are currently lacking."

"How long are you planning to be gone?"

"Don't know. It sort of depends on how Aunt Harriet is doing." There was no Aunt Harriet, of course, and he would have to have Doctor Bob or Myra take the cat to Mike's. Deirdre and Missy both smelled of dog, and Scott could no longer even stroke his old friend; Bill ran away if he came too near.

"What does he eat?"

"Friskies," Scott said. "And a

good supply will come with the animal. If I decide to go, that is."

"Okay, you got a deal."

"Thanks, Mike. You're a pal."

"I am, but not just because of that. You did this town a small but valuable mitzvah when you helped the McComb woman get up so she could finish the race. What was happening with her and her wife was ugly. It's better now."

"A *little* better."

"Actually quite a lot."

"Well, thanks. And Happy New Year again."

"Back atcha, buddy. What's the feline's name?"

"Bill. Bill D. Cat, actually."

"Like in *Bloom County.* Cool."

"Pick him up and give him a

stroke once in awhile. If I decide to go, that is. He likes that."

Scott hung up, thought about what giving things away meant — especially things that were also valued friends — and closed his eyes.

Doctor Bob called a few days later, and asked Scott if his weight-loss was remaining constant at one and a half to two pounds a day. Scott said it was, knowing the lie couldn't come back to haunt him; he looked the same as ever, right down to the bulge of belly hanging over his belt.

"So . . . you still think you'll be down to nothing in early March?"

"Yes."

Scott now thought Zero Day

might come before January was out, but he didn't know for sure, couldn't even make an educated guess, because he had stopped weighing himself. Not so long ago he had avoided the bathroom scale because it showed too many pounds; now he stayed away for the opposite reason. The irony was not lost on him.

For the time being Bob and Myra Ellis were not to know how things had speeded up, nor were Missy and Deirdre. He would have to tell them eventually, because when the end came, he would need help from one of them. And he knew which one.

"What do you weigh now?" Doctor Bob asked.

"106," Scott said.

"Holy shit!"

He guessed Ellis would say a lot more than holy shit if he knew what Scott knew: it was more like seventy. He could cross his big living room in four loping strides, or jump, catch one of the overhead beams, and swing from it like Tarzan. He hadn't reached what his weight would be on the moon, but he was closing in on it.

Doctor Bob was silent for a moment, then said, "Have you considered that the cause of what's happening to you might be alive?"

"Sure," Scott said. "Maybe an exotic bacteria that got into a cut, or some extremely rare virus that I inhaled."

"Has it crossed your mind that it might be sentient?"

It was Scott's turn to be silent. At last he said, "Yes."

"You're dealing with this extremely well, I must say."

"So far, so good," Scott said, but three days later he discovered just how much he might have to deal with before the end came. You thought you knew, you thought you could get ready . . . and then you tried to get the mail.

Western Maine had been experiencing a January thaw since New Year's Day, with temperatures in the fifties. Two days after Doctor Bob's call, it climbed all the way into the sixties, and the kids went back to school wearing their light jackets. That night, however, temperatures dropped and a sleety, granular snow began falling.

Scott barely noticed. He spent the evening on his computer, ordering stuff. He could have gotten all the items locally — the wheelchair and chest harness from the ostomy department of the CVS where he'd bought his Halloween candy, the ramp and clamps from Purdy's Hardware — but local people had a tendency to talk. And ask questions. He didn't want that.

The snow ended around midnight, and the following day dawned clear and cold. The new snow, frozen to a crust on top, was almost too brilliant to look at. It was as if his lawn and driveway had been sprayed with transparent plastic. Scott put on his parka and went out to get the mail. He had gotten in the habit of skipping the steps and just leaping down to the driveway. His legs, wildly overmuscled for his weight, seemed to crave that explosion of energy.

He did it now, and when his feet hit the icy crust, they shot out from under him. He landed on his ass, started to laugh, then stopped when he began to slide. He went down the slope of the lawn on his back, like a weight along the sawdusty surface of an arcade bowling game, gaining speed as he approached the street. He grabbed at a bush, but it was coated with ice and his hand slid off. He rolled over on his stomach and spread his legs, thinking that might slow him down. It didn't. He only slued sideways.

The crust is thick but not *that* thick, he thought. If I weighed as much as I look like I weigh, I'd break through and stop. But I don't. I'm going into the street, and if a car's coming along, it probably won't be able to stop in time. Then I won't have to worry about Zero Day.

He didn't go that far. He struck the post on which his mailbox was mounted, and hard enough to knock the wind out of him. When he recovered, he tried to stand up. He did a split on the slippery crust and went down again. He braced his feet against the post and pushed. That didn't work, either. He went four or five feet, his momentum died, and he slid back into the post. Next he tried pulling himself along, but his clutching fingers only slid on the crust. He had forgotten his gloves, and his hands were going numb.

I need help, he thought, and the name that immediately jumped to mind was Deirdre's. He reached into the pocket of his parka, but for once he had forgotten his phone. It was sitting back on his study desk. He supposed he could push himself into the street anyway, work his way over to the side, and wave down an oncoming car. Someone would stop and help him, but that someone would ask questions Scott didn't want to answer. His driveway was even more hopeless; it looked like a skating rink.

So here I am, he thought, like a turtle on its back. Hands going numb, feet soon to follow.

He craned to look up at the bare trees, their branches swaying mildly against the cloudless blue sky. He looked at the mailbox, and saw what might be a solution to his serio-comic problem. He sat up with his crotch braced against the post and grabbed the metal flag on the side of the box. It was loose, and two hard pulls was enough to snap it off. He used the ragged metal end to dig two holes in the crust. He put his knee in one, then his foot in the other. He stood up, holding the post with his free hand for balance. He made his way up the lawn to the steps in this fashion, bending to chop through the crust, stepping forward, then breaking through the crust again.

A couple of cars went by, and someone honked. Scott raised a hand and waved without turning around. By the time he got back to the steps, his hands had lost all feeling, and one was bleeding in two places. His back hurt like a motherfucker. He started up to the door, slipped, and barely managed to grab the ice-coated iron railing before he could go sliding back down to the mailbox again. He wasn't sure he would have had it in him to climb back up, even with holes to step in. He was exhausted, stinking with sweat inside his parka. He lay down in the hall. Bill came to look at him — but not *too* close — and miaowed his concern.

"I'm okay," he said. "Don't worry, you'll still get fed."

Yes, I'm okay, he thought. Just a little impromptu sledding on the crust. But this is where the really weird shit begins.

He supposed if there was a consolation, it was that the really weird shit wouldn't last long.

But I need to put up those clamps and put down that ramp ASAP. Not much time now.

On a Monday evening in mid-month, the members of the "Dr. Ellis party" had their last meal together. Scott hadn't seen any of them for a week, citing the need to hole up and finish his current department store project. Which had actually been done, at least in first draft, before Christmas. He guessed someone else would be applying the finishing touches.

He said it would have to be a potluck, with them bringing the food, because cooking had become difficult for him. In truth, everything had become difficult. Going upstairs was easy enough; three large, effortless leaps did the job. Going down was harder. He was afraid he might tumble and break a leg, so he held the railing and eased down step by step, like an old man with gout and bad hips. He had also developed a tendency to run into walls, because momentum had become hard to judge and even harder to control.

Myra asked him about the ramp now covering the steps to the stoop. Doctor Bob and Missy were more concerned about the wheelchair sitting in the corner of the living room, and the chest harness — made for people with little or no ability to sit upright — draped over its back. Deirdre asked no questions, only looked at him with wise, unhappy eyes.

They ate a tasty vegetarian casserole (Missy), au gratin potatoes with a cheesy sauce (Myra), and topped the meal off with a lumpy but tasty angel food cake that was only slightly burned on the bottom (Doctor Bob). The wine was good, but the talk and the laughter were better.

When they were finished, he said: "Time to fess up. I've been lying to you. This has been going quite a bit faster than I said it was."

"Scott, no!" Missy cried.

Doctor Bob nodded, seeming unsurprised. "How much faster?"

"Three pounds a day, not one or two."

"And how much do you weigh now?"

"I don't know. I've been avoiding the scale. Let's find out."

Scott tried to stand. His thighs

connected with the table and he flew forward, knocking over two wineglasses when he put out his hands to stop himself. Deirdre quickly picked up the tablecloth and threw it over the spill.

"Sorry, sorry," Scott said. "Don't know my own strength these days."

He turned as gingerly as a man on roller skates, and started toward the back half of the house. No matter how carefully he tried to walk, his steps became leaps. His remaining weight wanted him on the earth; his muscles insisted he rise above it. He overbalanced and had to grab one of the newly installed clamps to keep from going headlong into the hallway.

"Oh God," Deirdre said. "It must

be like learning to walk all over again."

You should have seen the last time I tried to get the mail, Scott thought. That was a *real* learning experience.

At least none of them were revisiting the clinic idea. Not that their failure to do that surprised him. A single look at his locomotion, at once awkward, ridiculous, and weirdly graceful, was enough to dispel the idea that a clinic might do him any good. This was a private matter now. They understood that. He was glad.

They all crowded into the bathroom and watched him stand on the Ozeri scale. "Jesus," Missy said quietly. "Oh, Scott."

The readout was 30.2 pounds.

He made his way back to the dining room with them following along behind. He went as carefully as a man using stones to cross a creek, and still ended up running into the table again. Missy instinctively reached out to steady him, but he waved her off before she could touch him.

When they were seated, he said, "I'm all right with this. Fine, in fact. Really."

Myra was very pale. "How can you be?"

"I don't know. I just am. But this is our farewell dinner. I won't see you guys again. Except for Deirdre. I need someone to help me at the end. Will you do it?"

"Yes, of course." She didn't hesitate, only put an arm around her wife, who had begun to cry.

"I just want to say . . ." Scott stopped, cleared his throat. "I want to say that I wish we had more time. You've been good friends to me."

"There's no compliment more sincere than that," Doctor Bob said. He was wiping his eyes with a napkin.

"It's not *fair*!" Missy burst out. "It's not goddam *fair*!"

"Well, no," Scott agreed, "it isn't. But I'm not leaving any kids behind, my ex is happy where she is, there's that, and it's fairer than cancer, or Alzheimer's, or being a burn victim in a hospital ward. I guess I'd go down in history, if anyone talked about it."

"Which we won't," Doctor Bob said.

"No," Deirdre agreed. "We won't. Can you tell me what it is you need me to do, Scott?"

He could and did, mentioning everything except what was tucked away in a paper bag in the hall closet. They listened in silence, and no one spoke a word of disagreement.

When he finished, Myra asked, very timidly, "What does it feel like, Scott? What do *you* feel like?"

Scott thought of how he'd felt running down Hunter's Hill, when he'd gotten his second wind and the whole world had stood revealed in the usually hidden glory of ordinary things — the leaden, lowering sky, the bunting flapping from the downtown buildings, every precious pebble and cigarette butt and beer can discarded by the side of the road. His own body for once working at top capacity, every cell loaded with oxygen.

"Elevated," he said at last.

He looked at Deirdre McComb, saw her shining eyes fixed on his face, and knew she understood why he had chosen her.

Myra coaxed Bill into his cat carrier. Doctor Bob took it down to his 4Runner and stowed it in the back. Then the four of them stood on the porch, their breath pluming in the cold night air. Scott remained in the entry, holding tight to one of the clamps.

"May I say something before we go?" Myra asked.

"Of course," Scott said, but wished she wouldn't. He wished they would just leave. He thought he had discovered one of life's great truths (and one he could have done without): the only thing harder than saying goodbye to yourself, a pound at a time, was saying goodbye to your friends.

"I was very foolish. I'm sorry about what's happening to you, Scott, but I'm glad about what's happened to me. If it hadn't, I would have stayed blind to some very good things, and some very good people. I would have stayed a foolish old woman. I can't hug you, so this will have to do."

She opened her arms, drew Deirdre and Missy to her, and embraced them. They hugged her back.

Doctor Bob said, "If you need me, I'll come at a sprint." He laughed. "Well, no, my sprinting days are actually behind me, but you know what I mean."

"I do," Scott said. "Thank you."

"So long, old man. Take care where you step. And how."

Scott watched them walk to Doctor Bob's car. He watched them get in. He waved, being careful to hold onto the clamp as he did it. Then he closed the door and made his half-walking, half-leaping way to the kitchen, feeling like a cartoon character. Which was, at bottom, the reason it felt so important to keep this a secret. He was sure he looked absurd, and it *was* absurd . . . but only if you were on the outside.

He sat down at the kitchen counter and looked at the empty corner where Bill's food and water dish had been for the last seven years. He looked at it for a long time. Then he went up to bed.

The following day, he got an email from Missy Donaldson.

I told DeeDee I wanted to go

with her, and be there at the end. We had quite an argument about it. I didn't give in until she reminded me about my foot, and how I felt about it when I was a young girl. I can run now — I love to run — but I was never a competition runner like DeeDee, because I'm only good for short distances, even after all these years. I was born with talipes equinovarus, you see, which is more commonly known as clubfoot. I had surgery to correct it when I was seven years old, but until then I walked with a cane, and it took me years afterward to learn to walk normally.

When I was four — I remember this very clearly — I showed my foot to my friend Felicity. She laughed and said it was a gross-ugly stupid foot. After that I didn't let anyone look at it except for my mother and the doctors. I didn't want people to laugh. DeeDee says that's how you feel about what's happening to you. She said, "He wants you to remember him the way he was when he was normal, not bouncing around in his house and looking like a bad special effect from a 1950s sci-fi movie."

Then I got it, but that doesn't mean I like it, or that you deserve it.

Scott, what you did the day of the race made it possible for us to stay in Castle Rock, not just because we have a business here but because now we can be a part of the town's greater life. DeeDee thinks she is going to be invited to join the Jaycees. She laughs and says it's silly, but I know that inside she doesn't think it's silly at all. It's a trophy, the same as the ones she got in the races she won. Oh, not everyone will accept us, I'm not so silly (or naive) as to believe that, some will never come around, but most will. Many already have. Without you that never would have happened, and without you, part of my beloved would always have remained closed off to the world. She won't tell you this, but I will: you knocked the chip off her shoulder. It was a big chip, and now she can walk straight again. She's always been a prickly pear, and I don't expect that to change, but she's open now. She sees more, hears more, can *be* more. You made that possible. You picked her up when she fell.

She says there's a bond between you, a shared feeling, and that's why she has to be the one to help you at the end. Am I jealous? A little, but I think I understand. It was when you said you felt elevated. She is that way when she runs. It's *why* she runs.

Please be brave, Scott, and

please know I am thinking of you. God bless.

All my love,
Missy

PS: When we go to the bookstore, we'll always pet Bill.

Scott thought about calling her and thanking her for saying such kind things, then decided that was a bad idea. It might get them both going. He printed out her note instead, and put it in one of the pockets of the harness.

He would take it with him when he went.

The following Sunday morning, Scott went along the hall to the downstairs bathroom in a series of steps that weren't steps at all. Each one was a long float that took him up to the ceiling, where he would push his tented fingers to bring himself back down. The furnace kicked on, and the soft whoosh of air from the vent actually blew him sideways a little. He twisted and grabbed a clamp to pull himself past the draft.

In the bathroom, he hovered over the scale and finally settled. At first he thought it wasn't going to report any weight at all. Then, at last, it coughed up a number: 2.1. It was about what he had expected.

That evening he called Deirdre's cell. He kept it simple. "I need you. Can you come?"

"Yes." It was all she said, and all he needed.

The door of the house was shut but unlocked. Deirdre slipped in, not opening the door all the way because of the draft. She turned on the hall lights to dispel the shadows, then went into the living room. Scott was in the wheelchair. He had managed to get partway into the harness, which had been buckled to the back of the chair, but his body floated upward from the chair's seat and one arm hung in the air. His face was bright with sweat, the front of his shirt dark with it.

"I almost waited too long," he said. He sounded breathless. "I had to swim down to the chair. Breast-stroke, if you can believe it."

Deirdre could. She went to him and stood in front of the wheel-chair, looking at him with wonder. "How long have you been here like this?"

"Awhile. Wanted to wait until dark. *Is* it dark?"

"Almost." She dropped to her knees. "Oh, Scott. This is so bad."

He shook his head back and forth in slow motion, like a man shaking his head underwater. "You know better."

She thought she did. Hoped she did.

He struggled with his floating arm and finally managed to shoot it into the vest's armhole. "Can you try to buckle the straps across my chest and waist without touching me?"

"I think so," she said, but twice her knuckles brushed him as she knelt in front of the chair — once his side, once his shoulder — and both times she felt her body rise and then settle back. Her stomach did a flip with each contact, what she remembered her father calling a whoops-my-dear when their car went over a big bump. Or, yes — Missy had been right — like when a rollercoaster crested the first hill, hesitated, then plunged.

At last it was done. "Now what?"

"Soon we sample the night air. But first go into the closet, the one in the entry where I keep my boots. There's a paper bag, and a coil of rope. I think you can push the wheelchair, but if you can't, you'll have to tie the rope around the headrest and pull it."

"And you're sure about this?"

He nodded, smiling. "Do you think I want to spend the rest of my life tied into this thing? Or having someone climb a stepladder to feed me?"

"Well, that would make a dandy YouTube video."

"One no one would believe."

She found the rope and the brown paper bag and took them back to the living room. Scott held out his hands. "Come on, big girl, let's see your skills. Toss me the bag from there."

She did, and it was a good throw.

The bag arced through the air toward his outreached hands . . . stopped less than an inch above his palms . . . then settled slowly into them. There the bag seemed to gain weight, and Deirdre had to remind herself of what he'd said when he first explained what was happening: things were heavy to *him.* Was that a paradox? It made her head hurt, whatever it was, and there was no time to think about it now, anyway. He stripped off the paper bag and held a square object wrapped in thick paper decorated with starbursts. Protruding from the bottom was a flat red tongue about six inches long.

"It's called a SkyLight. A hundred and fifty dollars from Fireworks

Factory in Oxford. I bought it online. Hope it's worth it."

"How will you light it? How can you, when . . . when you're . . ."

"Don't know if I can, but confidence is high. It's got a scratch fuse."

"Scott, do I have to do this?"

"Yes," he said.

"You want to go."

"Yes," he said. "It's time."

"It's cold outside, and you're covered with sweat."

"It doesn't matter."

But it did to her. She went upstairs to his bedroom and pulled the comforter off a bed that had been slept in — at some point, anyway — but bore no impression of his body on the mattress or his head on the pillow.

"Comforter," she snorted. It seemed a very stupid word under the circumstances. She took it downstairs and tossed it to him as she had tossed the paper bag, watching with the same fascination as it paused . . . bloomed . . . and then settled over his chest and lap.

"Wrap that around you."

"Yes, ma'am."

She watched him do it, then tucked the part trailing on the floor under his feet. This time the lift was more serious, the whoops-my-dear a double flip instead of a single. Her knees rose from the floor and she could feel her hair stream upward. Then it was done, and when her knees thumped down on the boards again, she had a better understanding of why he could smile. She remembered something she'd read in college — Faulkner, maybe: *Gravity is the anchor that pulls us down into our graves.* There would be no grave for this man, and no more gravity, either. He had been given a special dispensation.

"Snug as a bug in a rug," he said.

"Don't joke, Scott. Please."

She went behind the wheelchair and put her hands tentatively on the jutting handles. There was no need of the rope; her weight stayed. She pushed him toward the door, onto the stoop, and down the ramp.

The night was cold, chilling the sweat on his face, but the air was as sweet and crisp as the first bite of a fall apple. Above him was a half-moon and what seemed like a trillion stars.

To match the trillion pebbles, just as mysterious, that we walk over every day, he thought. Mystery above, mystery below. Weight, mass, reality: mystery all around.

"Don't you cry," he said. "This isn't a goddam funeral."

She pushed him onto the snowy lawn. The wheels sank eight inches deep and stopped. Not far from the house, but far enough to avoid being caught under one of the eaves. That *would* be an anticlimax, he thought, and laughed.

"What's the joke, Scott?"

"Nothing," he said. "Everything."

"Look down there. At the street."

Scott saw three bundled-up figures, each with a flashlight: Missy, Myra, and Doctor Bob.

"I couldn't keep them away." Deirdre came around the wheelchair and dropped to one knee in front of the bundled-up figure with his bright eyes and sweat-clumped hair.

"Did you try? Tell the truth, DeeDee." It was the first time he had called her that.

"Well . . . not very hard."

He nodded and smiled. "Good discussion."

She laughed, then wiped her eyes. "Are you ready?"

"Yes. Can you help me with the buckles?"

She managed the two holding the harness to the back of the chair, and he rose at once against the lap strap. She had to struggle with that, because it was tight and her hands were going numb in the January cold. She kept touching him, and each time she did her body would rise from the snow cover, making her feel like a human pogo stick. She stuck with it, and finally the last strap holding him to the chair began to slide free.

"I love you, Scott," she said. "We all do."

"Right back atcha," he said. "Give your good girl a kiss for me."

"Two," she promised.

Then the strap slithered out of the buckle and it was done.

■ ■ ■ ■

He rose slowly from the chair, the coverlet trailing below him like the hem of a long skirt, feeling absurdly like Mary Poppins, minus the umbrella. Then a breeze caught him, and he began to rise faster. He clutched the coverlet with one hand and the SkyLight against his chest with the other. He saw the diminishing circle of Deirdre's upturned face. He watched her wave, but his hands were occupied and he couldn't wave back. He saw the others wave from where they stood on View Drive. He saw their flashlights focused on him, and noted how they began drawing together as he gained altitude.

The breeze tried to turn him, making him think of how he'd slued sideways on his ridiculous trip down his snow-crusted lawn to the mailbox, but when he partially unwrapped the coverlet and held it out on the side the wind was coming from, he steadied. That might not last long, but it didn't matter. For the time being he only wanted to look down and see his friends — Deirdre on the lawn by the wheelchair, the others in the street. He passed his bedroom window and saw the lamp was still on, casting a yellow stripe on his bed. He could see things on his bureau — watch, comb, little fold of money — that he would never touch again. He rose higher, and the moonlight was bright enough for him to see some kid's Frisbee caught in an angle of the roof, maybe tossed up there before he and Nora had bought the place.

That kid could be grown up now, he thought. Writing in New York or digging ditches in San Francisco or painting in Paris. Mystery, mystery, mystery.

Now he caught escaping heat from the house, a thermal, and began rising faster. The town disclosed itself as if from a drone or low-flying plane, the streetlamps along Main Street and Castle View like pearls on a string. He could see the Christmas tree that Deirdre had lit over a month ago, and which would remain in the town square until the first of February.

It was cold up here, much colder than on the ground, but that was all right. He let the coverlet go and watched it drop, spreading out as it went, slowing, becoming a parachute, not weightless but almost.

Everyone should have this, he thought, and perhaps, at the end, everyone does. Perhaps in their time of dying, everyone rises.

He held out the SkyLight and scratched the fuse with a fingernail. Nothing happened.

Light, damn you. I didn't get much of a last meal, so could I at least have a last wish?

He scratched again.

"I can't see him anymore," Missy

said. She was crying. "He's gone. We might as well —"

"Wait," Deirdre said. She had joined them at the foot of Scott's driveway.

"For what?" Doctor Bob asked.

"Just wait."

So they waited, looking up into the darkness.

"I don't think —" Myra began.

"A little longer," Deirdre said, thinking, Come on, Scott, come on, you're almost at the finish line, it's your race to win, your tape to break through, so don't blow it. Don't choke. Come on, big boy, let's see your skills.

Brilliant fire burst high above them: reds and yellows and greens. There was a pause, then came a perfect fury of gold, a shimmering waterfall that rained down and rained down and rained down, as if it would never end.

Deirdre took Missy's hand.

Doctor Bob took Myra's hand.

They watched until the last golden sparks went out, and the night was dark again. Somewhere high above them, Scott Carey continued to gain elevation, rising above the earth's mortal grip with his face turned toward the stars.

ABOUT THE AUTHOR

Stephen King is the author of more than fifty books, all of them worldwide bestsellers. His recent work includes *The Outsider, Sleeping Beauties* (cowritten with his son Owen King), the short story collection *The Bazaar of Bad Dreams,* the Bill Hodges trilogy *End of Watch, Finders Keepers,* and *Mr. Mercedes* (an Edgar Award winner for Best Novel and now an AT&T Audience Network original television series),

Doctor Sleep, and *Under the Dome.*
His novel *11/22/63* — a Hulu original television series event — was
named a top ten book of 2011 by
the *New York Times Book Review*
and won the *Los Angeles Times*
Book Prize for Mystery/Thriller.
His epic works *The Dark Tower* and
It are the basis for major motion
pictures. He is the recipient of the
2018 PEN America Literary Service Award, the 2014 National
Medal of Arts, and the 2003 National Book Foundation Medal for
Distinguished Contribution to
American Letters. He lives in Ban-
gor, Maine, with his wife, novelist
Tabitha King.

The employees of Thorndike Press hope you have enjoyed this Large Print book. All our Thorndike, Wheeler, and Kennebec Large Print titles are designed for easy reading, and all our books are made to last. Other Thorndike Press Large Print books are available at your library, through selected bookstores, or directly from us.

For information about titles, please call:
(800) 223-1244

or visit our website at:
gale.com/thorndike

To share your comments, please write:
Publisher
Thorndike Press
10 Water St., Suite 310
Waterville, ME 04901